For Jim Ellis,
a friend for many lifetimes

Gallows
Hill

PROLOGUE

The crystal paperweight should have been clear, but it was not. The man who had cast it was bewildered. He was certain that he had used the correct amount of selenium to counteract the iron in the silica sand and decolorize the glass. He had been in the glass-pressing business all his life and took great pride in the quality of his work.

Still, when he peered into the globe, which by rights should have been clear and transparent as window glass, he saw at its core what appeared to be gray wisps of smoke, twisting and curling, rising and darting, twining and intertwining like a nest of snakes preparing to strike.

With a sigh of regret he consigned the paperweight to a bin of defective glass products labeled Seconds. Eventually the crystal sphere, along with a sad assortment of hornless unicorns, tuskless elephants, and double-beaked swans, was placed on a special shelf of curios at the back of the showroom.

A surprising number of people made it a habit to browse the discount shelf in search of bargains and joke presents. One of those customers was an older woman with thick black hair and heavy-lidded eyes. She picked up the paperweight and examined it carefully, more than a little disturbed by what she saw in its depths. In fact the images she found there upset her so much that she left the shop without making a purchase.

The following day she came back and found the ball still on the shelf. This time she forced herself to buy it. When she got home, she took a seat in a straight-backed chair in a dimly lit room, placed the globe on a black velvet cloth on a table in front of her, and looked once more at the visions that appeared in the swirling mists. Being practiced in the ways of scrying, she knew what they meant and set about putting her affairs in order.

Ten days later, when she suffered a fatal heart attack, her house was clean, her bills were paid, and her will had been updated.

The woman's son flew in from California for the funeral and put the small house up for sale. Since he was soon to be married, he had thought he might keep the furniture, but when he saw the condition of the mismatched chairs and the underslung sofa with cigarette burns in the upholstery, he sold them too, getting less than a hundred dollars for the lot. He gave his mother's strange, wild clothes to charity, but took her personal effects home with him for sentiment's sake.

Among those items was the paperweight, which he placed on a corner of his desk, where it remained for the rest of his comparatively short lifetime, clear and transparent as window glass.

chapter
ONE

The first time Sarah Zoltanne saw Eric Garrett, he was standing out by the flagpole in front of the school building talking with a group of friends. Backlit as he was by the afternoon sunlight, everything about him seemed painted in gold—his hair, his skin, and, as far as she could tell from where she stood some distance away at the top of the cement steps, it even appeared that he might have golden eyes. In her literature class back in California she had done a unit on mythology, and the image that leaped immediately into her mind was of Apollo.

From then on Sarah seemed to keep seeing him everywhere. Striding down the hall between classes with an armload of books. Seated in the bleachers with some of the guys from the football team watching cheerleader practice. Pulling out of the student parking lot behind the wheel of a red Dodge Charger filled with laughing teenagers. She was actually starting to wonder if Fate was trying to tell her something, when he turned up behind the podium at a senior-class assembly. Only then did she

3

realize that he was president of the class. Since she herself was on the lowest rung of the social ladder, having just started as a transfer student in her senior year, she saw no point in further speculation.

Which was why she was taken totally by surprise when, one Thursday afternoon in late October, she arrived at her locker at the end of fourth period to find the Sun God standing there waiting for her.

"Hi," he said. "We don't know each other, but it's time we did. I'm Eric Garrett."

"I know who you are," Sarah said. "I've seen you at assemblies." She wondered what on earth he could possibly want. She already had learned the hard way that the "in" crowd at Pine Crest High School didn't waste time on outsiders, especially on one who arrived under the circumstances she had. It occurred to her that he might be keynoting one of those degrading "Be Kind to New Students" programs, the kind that gave extra credit for being nice to newcomers. In her last school she had been so embarrassed for the new students that her natural friendly impulses had been immediately quelled.

"I know who you are too," Eric said with a contagious twinkle. "You're Sarah Zoltanne. You're from Ventura, California. You and your mother moved here at the end of August. I know more. Ready? Your favorite food is— this is hard to believe—artichokes! You're hooked on New Age music, and you've got a black cat named Yowler with a torn left ear."

"Where did you hear all that?" Sarah asked in astonishment.

He grinned. "What would you say if I told you a psychic told me?"

4

"I'd say you're pulling my leg. Pine Crest is not exactly a hot spot for metaphysics."

"You're a smart girl," Eric said. "I see you've got your thumb on the pulse of this town, and you've only just got here. So you can see how we're going to have a pretty rough time digging up a psychic in this community. How would *you* like to be one Saturday night?"

"What's happening Saturday night?" His eyes weren't really gold, she decided; they were hazel with golden flecks, like sun-speckled pond water, and his lashes were long and light, the exact same shade as his eyebrows.

"The Halloween Carnival. You must have seen the posters. Every year the senior class puts on a carnival to earn money to hire a band for the prom in the spring. There're contests, games, a spook house, and all that stuff. I was hoping to talk you into being the fortune-teller."

"I don't know a thing about telling fortunes," Sarah said.

"There's nothing to it," Eric said reassuringly. "You just read people's palms or whatever and tell them their future."

"There's no way anybody can know the future."

"No, of course not. So you'd just make things up, like they're going to find money or take a trip or meet somebody sexy and irresistible. Nobody's going to sue you if the predictions don't pan out."

"I wouldn't know where to start," Sarah said. "I don't know anything about anybody in Pine Crest."

"That's what makes this idea so great and you so perfect," Eric explained. "The kids here don't know you either. The main reason there's never been a fortune-

5

telling booth at the carnival is because nobody wants to spend money having their fortunes told by somebody they've known since kindergarten. But it would be different if it were done by a stranger."

Sarah had to struggle to hide her disappointment. For a few lovely minutes in the beginning she had actually thought that he might be getting ready to ask her for a date. But her first assumption had been correct. He had only sought her out because he wanted something from her.

"I wouldn't be any good at that," she said.

"Don't say no until you've heard me out," Eric quickly countered. "I've got this dynamite system that will make it a cinch for you. You'll dress like a Gypsy—we can borrow a costume from the Drama Club—and under your scarf you'll wear earphones. On the other side of the room we'll station an accomplice with a hidden walkie-talkie. When she sees people enter your tent, she'll secretly fill you in on their background. You'll look at their palms and tell each person their whole life story so that they'll think you are reading their minds! It'll blow them away!"

"How will my accomplice know so much?"

"Kyra's a walking encyclopedia," Eric said. "Her parents were born and raised here, and she knows all the dirt about everybody. She'll feed you so much info, you won't know what to do with it all."

"Oh, so Kyra's behind this," Sarah said stiffly. The pieces of the puzzle flew quickly together and made sickening sense to her. No wonder Eric knew so many things about her, including the tattered condition of Yowler's poor ear! She shuddered to think of what other information Kyra might have given him about personal things

6

that were none of his business. Did he know which de-odorant she used? What brand of toothpaste? Did he know that she broke out in hives whenever she ate chocolate? Did he know that ever since she and Rosemary had moved to Pine Crest, she had experienced nightmares so dreadful that she cried out in her sleep? I can't bear it, she thought. Not this on top of everything else. How dare that horrid girl make my private life public!

She managed to keep her voice steady and said politely, "No, thank you. I appreciate being asked, but I don't want to tell fortunes."

"Come on, be a sport!" He said it in a way that implied he seemed to think she wanted to be coaxed. "Think what a great way this will be for you to meet people. By the time the evening's over, you'll know everybody in town."

"I don't want to do it," Sarah repeated. "Especially not if it involves Kyra. And as for knowing everybody in Pine Crest, that doesn't really matter. I'm not going to spend my life here, it's just for one year. Now, please, excuse me, but I've got to get a move on. If I don't get going, I'll be late for P.E."

She took off down the hall so fast that she was almost running, half expecting to feel a restraining hand on her sleeve or to hear Eric calling her name as he hurried after her. It was not until she was almost at the end of the hall that she realized she hadn't gotten her gym clothes out of her locker. She briefly considered going back for them and decided against it. Eric had seemed so self-confident that she might well find him still standing there, waiting for her to return to say she'd changed her mind.

She would tell the coach she had forgotten that her

gym clothes were in the laundry, accept a demerit, and chalk up one more victory to Kyra. At least, she told herself with some satisfaction, she had the comfort of knowing that she had handled an awkward situation with dignity. Thank goodness it had not turned out to be "Be Kind to New Students Week" after all.

"You shouldn't have asked her!" Kyra exclaimed. "It's not like you *had* to. If you were that hard up for a fortune-teller, you could have asked *me*! I would have been glad to do it."

"You're a junior," Eric said. "The carnival's a senior-class project. Juniors aren't allowed to participate, except to help with the promotion."

They were standing in the school entrance hall, just to the left of the open doorway through which the entire student body was trying to cram itself at once. Kyra was acutely aware of the picture they made together, with Eric, as tall and blond as the hero in a romance novel, and she, small, snub-nosed, and freckled, with a head of orange curls that came barely to the level of his shoulder. She was conscious, too, of the lack of curious glances from the students streaming past them. Everybody was so used to seeing the two of them together that nobody took it for anything more than a platonic friendship that dated back to preschool days when their mothers, who had been best friends since high school, had traded them back and forth as if they were cousins.

"So what if I'm a junior?" she asked, keeping the tone light. "That didn't stop you from asking me to man the walkie-talkie."

"That's different," Eric said. "Nobody would have known you were doing it. And even if you were a senior, you're just not the type to play a Gypsy. Gypsies are dark and mysterious, not red-haired pixies."

"What's so mysterious about Sarah?" Kyra demanded. "It's not like she comes from some weird place like Romania. Ventura is a California beach town full of stuck-up weirdos who call their parents by their first names and listen to recordings of people beating drums and chanting."

"People around here don't know where she's from," Eric reminded her. "Her name sounds foreign and exotic, and she looks like a Gypsy with that long black hair and those bedroom eyes."

"Why not use Debbie Rice?" Kyra suggested. "She's got dark hair, and her eyes are as bedroomy as you can get. On top of that, she's president of the Drama Club, so she ought to be able to pull it off."

"I don't want Debbie," Eric said stubbornly. "I want the Zoltanne girl. Doesn't your dad hang around for student conferences on Thursdays? Let's see if we can catch him before he takes off."

"What do you want from my father?" Kyra asked in surprise. "You can't think *Dad* has any influence over Sarah!"

"He might. He's used to having people do what he tells them. And after all, he's on the way to becoming her stepfather."

"Don't count on it!" Kyra snapped. "It's a middle-age fling, that's all! Besides, the first thing Dad will ask us is if Mr. Prue's okayed it. Almost everybody on the school board is on the governing board of the church, and you know how they feel about anything that smacks of the occult. It was hard enough to convince them just to let us have a spook house."

9

"Gypsies aren't *occult,*" Eric said. "They're a bunch of beggars who look at the lines in people's hands and make up stories about them. Besides, we don't have to tell him what sort of booth it will be. We'll just say we'd like to have Sarah on the Carnival Committee and we need his help in convincing her. Come on, Carrot Top, let's go have a talk with him. We need that carnival money to finance the prom."

"I probably won't even get to the prom," Kyra said. "Juniors can't go unless they're dating seniors."

"I wouldn't be surprised if a senior asked you," Eric told her. "Stranger things have been known to happen." He flashed her his white-gold grin, and a dimple appeared in one cheek, giving him the look of a mischievous ten-year-old.

As always, Kyra felt herself melting.

"All right, I'll go with you to talk to him," she said reluctantly. "I warn you, though, it's not going to do any good. Sarah hates my father as much as I hate Rosemary. My dad doesn't have any pull with her at all."

chapter
TWO

The house they had rented on Windsor Street was a small, one-story stucco structure with blue wooden trim. The front yard was almost totally devoid of grass because a huge oak tree had kept it shaded throughout the summer. Now the tree was losing its leaves, and sunlight slipped between its branches to fall in erratic patterns on the ground below, mottling the surface with patches of light and shadow.

Her mother had raked that day, Sarah noted as she crossed the yard to the house. It was probably as good a way for her to keep busy as any. In Ventura they had lived in a garden apartment. The landlord had been responsible for keeping the grounds up. But there, of course, her mother had held a full-time job and had not had any time to devote to yard work.

Yowler was perched on the doorstep, slit-eyed and glaring, looking like a displaced alien. When Sarah opened the door, he continued to crouch there, defiantly expressing his lack of interest, until the very last moment before the door closed, when he slid in after her and disappeared behind an armchair.

Sarah sympathized totally. She, too, had a feeling that she should have rung the bell before entering. Although they had been living here for over two months, she still felt like a visitor in somebody else's home. Her mother had made an effort to lay claim to the place by painting the walls the same shade of eggshell white as those in their last apartment, so that their furniture was set against a familiar backdrop, but the proportions of the rooms were so different that nothing seemed to fit or to look like it belonged there.

The house smelled of chocolate. Sarah crossed the living room to the kitchen, where her mother was removing a pan of brownies from the oven.

Rosemary Zoltanne glanced up with a welcoming smile. She was dressed in jeans and a bright red sweatshirt. Her soft, pale hair was combed back from her face and tied with a scarlet ribbon, giving her the look of a child at a Christmas party.

"Hi, honey," she said. "I didn't hear you come in. Did you stop to admire the job I did on the yard?"

"You must have used a vacuum cleaner," Sarah said. "What's with the brownies? You know I don't eat chocolate, and we've still got half the spice cake you baked on Tuesday."

"I wanted to make something special for the weekend," her mother said, straightening up and setting the pan on the counter. "You can eat the cake while Kyra and Brian eat brownies. Something for everybody, right?"

"They're coming again? We just got rid of them!"

"I don't like to hear you talk like that," Rosemary said.

12

"They probably won't sleep over, since they stayed both nights last weekend, but I'm sure they'll be spending some time here. Ted wants to see as much of his kids as he can." She paused and then deliberately switched gears. "So, how was school?" she asked brightly. "Did you talk to the sponsor of the Drama Club?"

"I told you the club's filled up. They don't have room for another member."

"I'm sure they'll make an exception for you," Rosemary said. "Especially when they find out how active you were in the drama club at your old school. Ted will talk to the sponsor if you feel awkward doing it."

"I don't want Ted pulling strings for me," Sarah said. "I put my name on the sign-up sheet and got turned down. As far as I'm concerned, that's the end of the story."

Leaving her mother to continue her culinary activities, she carried her books down the hall to her bedroom. Although it was close to the size of her room in Ventura, it seemed much smaller because of the extra bed. Her beloved, double-size waterbed was stored in the garage along with most of their other belongings until such time as her mother and Ted got married and bought a house. "After we're married" was her mother's favorite phrase these days, as though the date of the wedding were firmly set. Until it took place—if indeed it ever did take place—and the "nice big house with four bedrooms" became a reality, the tiny room off the kitchen was allocated to Brian, and Sarah's room was also Kyra's on weekends or whenever else she decided she wanted to sleep over. Even on nights when Sarah had the room to herself, it didn't feel like it belonged to her, with Kyra's bed positioned across from her own and two whole drawers of the bureau assigned to Kyra, even though she kept nothing there except pajamas.

Sarah shut the door and dumped her books on her desk, pausing as she did so to switch on her tape player. As the soothing strains of woodwinds and wind chimes filled the room, she threw herself down on her bed and closed her eyes. The remainder of the afternoon stretched drearily before her. Back home she had been involved in so many activities, what with club meetings, play rehearsals, beach parties, and trips to the mall, that the days had never been long enough to get everything done. Here she had nothing to occupy her time except schoolwork, which took a minimum of effort, since Pine Crest High was not as advanced as her school in California. Perhaps she should look into finding an after-school job, she thought. It would be nice to have spending money of her own again. Now that Rosemary wasn't working, cash was tight, and when Ted had offered to give Sarah an allowance, she had refused it. There was no way she was going to be indebted to Ted Thompson for anything more than she absolutely had to be.

The irony of it was that if she had played her cards right, she could have kept her mother from meeting him. The complaint of a sore throat or even a bad headache would have done it. All she'd had to do was say she didn't feel well and Rosemary never would have left her to go to San Francisco. Still, there was no way she could have known what would happen there. For years her career-oriented mother had been attending educational conferences in the summer while Sarah was at camp or staying with one of her girlfriends, and she always had come home stimulated and revitalized, ready to plunge back into her teaching schedule in the fall.

How could Sarah have guessed that this time it would be different? She couldn't have, of course, and yet there had been something—she couldn't exactly call it a premonition, but *something.*

That "something" had caused her to wonder for a moment about her eyesight. It had happened the evening before her mother's departure when she had passed by the open door of Rosemary's bedroom and seen a flash of yellow in the mirror over the dresser. The room had been dimly illuminated by light from the hallway, and when Sarah stepped back to peer into it, she saw nothing more than the shadowy reflection of herself—a tall, slim girl with a mane of black hair, who was dressed in a white, sleeveless T-shirt and hot pink jogging shorts.

It was odd, she had thought, and she felt disconcerted but not particularly concerned. She hoped this didn't mean she was going to need glasses. She turned to start back down the hall, and saw it again—at the edge of her line of vision, a glimpse of something yellow. This time she entered the room and turned on the overhead lights, only to find nothing yellow anywhere in sight. It wasn't until her mother returned from the conference and Sarah was chatting with her while she unpacked that she saw the full-skirted, sunflower-colored cocktail dress.

"Is that new?" she asked.

"I bought it in San Francisco," Rosemary told her. "I didn't pack the right clothes. I forgot to take something dressy to go out to dinner in."

"They wouldn't let you into a restaurant in a suit?"

"Sure, but who wants to go dancing in something tailored?" Her mother's voice held a lilt that was almost girlish.

"Dancing?" Sarah said slowly. "You went out dancing?"

"There are all sorts of wonderful dance clubs in San Francisco." Rosemary was facing the closet as she spoke, and the statement was tossed back over her shoulder in a careless manner, but when she turned from placing the yellow dress on a padded hanger, her face had a glow that made the words seem magical.

"Who was this guy?" Sarah asked her.

"His name's Ted Thompson."

"An English teacher?"

"Who else would a person meet at a convention of English teachers?"

"Available?"

She expected her mother to say, "Of course," but instead she paused and then said hesitantly, "Well, sort of."

"Sort of?"

"He and his wife are separated. They're in the process of getting a divorce, but it hasn't come through yet. He's a very special man, so attractive, and unbelievably thoughtful. He said he'd call tonight to make sure I got home all right, can you imagine?"

As if on cue the telephone rang.

"I'll get it!" Rosemary exclaimed, and went dashing to answer it. "Oh, hi!" Sarah heard her trill. "Yes, fine, it was a very smooth flight! . . . Nothing much, in fact we've just finished dinner. . . . We—my daughter and I—who did you think I meant? . . . No, I'm afraid I've had more than my quota of seafood in the past few evenings. Not that I didn't love it, but Hamburger Helper is more the norm around here." A pause and a giggle. "Yes, it was, wasn't it?" A longer pause. "Me too. . . . Yes, really. I can't say it now, but I do. I'll talk to you tomorrow, then. Sleep well, Ted."

The receiver clicked back in place, and Rosemary sighed.

After that Ted Thompson's phone calls came on the dot of eight every evening. Then he arrived in person, and that was a shock. Far from the Harrison Ford type that Sarah had been anticipating, her mother's "boyfriend" (Rosemary's term, not Sarah's) turned out to be a humorless, square-jawed man with horn-rimmed glasses and a head of rust-colored hair that was streaked with gray. Sarah could not imagine what Rosemary saw in him. Widowed for over twelve years, her mother had attracted plenty of men, and if she had wanted to remarry she could certainly have done so. Instead she had never shown the slightest interest in anything more than casual dating and had seemed quite content to devote herself to motherhood and her teaching career.

When Ted arrived in her life, that sensible, down-to-earth Rosemary vanished, to be replaced by a starry-eyed stranger who made senseless decisions. Although Ted started out sleeping on the sofa in the living room, by his third night there he was sharing the master bedroom. By the time the long week was over, it had already been decided that Rosemary would give notice at the school where she taught and that she and Sarah would follow him back to Missouri.

Now, as she often did, Sarah blocked that memory from her consciousness and let herself pretend that the move hadn't happened. It had all been a silly dream, and if she didn't accept its validity, she was bound to wake up and find herself still in California, where the scents

17

of summer lingered in the damp salt air of October and crimson hibiscus bloomed in front of their garden apartment. The cries of gulls would replace the harsh caws of crows. And the clouds would be puffy and white and blow in off the ocean like cotton balls, not dull, striated layers spread out like thin sheets of plastic against the sky behind Garrett Hill, whose pine-covered slopes gave the town of Pine Crest its name. When the phone rang, the calls would not be from Sheila, Ted's soon-to-be ex-wife, whining about how lonely she was or begging Ted to come over and repair her dishwasher, but from longtime pals like Gillian or Ryan or Lindsay—or from *Jon,* who had been on the verge of being more than a "friend"—each one wanting to know if Sarah was free to party or to go to the beach or a movie or just out cruising.

She was zipping along the beach road in the backseat of Ryan's Jeep, with her head tipped back against Jon's shoulder, roaring with laughter at one of his crazy surfing stories, when a knock at the bedroom door caused her eyes to fly open. To her surprise she discovered the afternoon was over. The tape had long since played itself out, and the room was heavy with silence and bathed in the glow of softening twilight.

"Sarah?" The voice was her mother's. "Will you come out here, please? There's something Ted and I feel we need to discuss with you."

"Okay," Sarah called back. "I'll be with you in a minute."

Her voice was foggy with sleep, and her limbs felt leaden. She realized that she must have been sleeping like a dead thing if Ted had managed to come home and she hadn't heard him. He always made a point of parking at the side of the house instead of in the driveway next to her mother's car, under the ridiculous assumption that if his own car wasn't visible from the street, nobody would suspect that he spent his nights there.

When she dragged herself to her feet and went out to the living room, she found Ted on the sofa munching brownies, with a worried-looking Rosemary seated next to him. It was obvious to Sarah that they had been discussing her, for the moment she appeared, her mother said, "Don't tell me you've been sleeping!"

"All right, I won't tell you," Sarah said. "I'll let you guess."

"Why? Are you sick?"

"Since when is napping a crime?"

"Excessive sleeping is a sign of depression," Ted said in the classroom-lecture voice that Sarah found so irritating.

"It's also a sign of boredom," Rosemary said, frowning. "Honey, it isn't healthy for you to spend all your afternoons closed up in your bedroom. You've got to start getting involved in some after-school activities."

"I was thinking of maybe getting a job," Sarah told her.

"I'd rather see you out doing things with friends."

"What friends?" Sarah snapped. "All my friends are in California!"

"There are plenty of nice kids here who could be your friends," Ted said. "Kyra stopped by my office today with Eric Garrett. He told me he asked you to help with the Halloween Carnival and you turned him down."

"Why would he come to you about that?" asked Sarah.

"He wanted my help in getting you to change your mind."

"Well, you can't," Sarah said. "I don't want to run the fortune-telling booth."

"Are they going to have a fortune-teller?" Ted seemed surprised. "I would have expected the school board to have raised an objection."

"Well, I think it sounds like fun," Rosemary said with enthusiasm. "Sarah, with your background in drama you could do that beautifully! And I know just the thing you can use for a crystal ball!"

"I don't want to be in the carnival," Sarah said stubbornly. "Is this what you called me out here for, or is dinner ready?"

"Your mother and I are going out to dinner," Ted said. "It's the four-month anniversary of the day we met."

"You're more than welcome to come with us—" Rosemary began.

"Another time," Ted interrupted. "Tonight is a special occasion, a celebration for the two of us. There's plenty of lasagna left over from last night's dinner."

"That's fine with me," Sarah said sarcastically. "It would be a shame to let dried-out lasagna go to waste."

She turned on her heel and started back to her bedroom.

"Sarah—" her mother called after her.

"Rosie, don't," Ted said, cutting off the plea. "You know she's only trying to wreck our evening. You mustn't keep letting yourself be manipulated this way. Our kids have got to adjust to the fact that our relationship is important to us and that we have to be allowed time alone together to cement it."

You're the one who's wrecked things, Sarah longed to fire back at him. *Rosemary and I had a great life back in Ventura!*

She choked back the words, however, and kept on walking, knowing that nothing she said would have any effect on him and not wanting to upset her mother any more than she had already. Once back in her bedroom, she left the door open to prevent any accusation from Ted that she was in there sulking. Turning on the light and taking a seat at the desk, she set about doing her algebra assignment.

She could hear her mother and Ted getting ready for their night on the town, as if eating at a Pine Crest restaurant were something to get excited about. The toilet flushed, water gushed through the rattling shower pipes, and her mother's hair dryer buzzed in harmony with Ted's electric razor. Finally the preparations were completed, and Sarah could hear the two of them arguing out in the living room about whether or not her mother should come back to say good night and tell her how many minutes to microwave the lasagna. As always, Ted won. The front door shut with a firm click, and a few minutes later Ted's car roared to life outside her window.

When the sound of the engine was finally lost in the distance, Sarah felt a release from tension that left her as limp and exhausted as if the stress had been physical. She considered heating up dinner—it was past seven-thirty—but she didn't feel hungry enough to make the effort.

By now she had finished the algebra, and with no other class to study for except American history, which she liked to postpone until bedtime so that she could read herself to sleep, she was faced with an evening as empty as the afternoon had been. The only thing she could think of to do was watch television, which she seldom did these days since the TV set was in the living room and it made her uncomfortable to sit there with her mother and Ted cuddling on the sofa like teenagers.

Now, with the house to herself, Sarah switched on the set and was flicking the dial in an aimless exploration of channels when the telephone rang. She was tempted not to answer it since she was sure it wasn't for her, but when it kept on ringing persistently, she gave in.

"Hello," she said, her eyes on the flickering TV screen.

"Is that you, Sarah?" The voice was all too familiar.

"Your father's not here," Sarah said. "They're out for the evening."

"I'm not calling Dad," Kyra said. "You're the one I want to talk to. Eric says the reason you won't do the fortune-telling thing is because I'm part of it."

"He told you right," Sarah said. "That shouldn't surprise you. You and I aren't exactly the best of friends."

"No, we're not," Kyra conceded. "But Eric and I *are.* We've known each other all our lives, and he's a cool guy, and I don't want to let him down. As for you and me, like it or not, we're stuck with the disgusting fact that our parents are having a—a—" She paused, and then with obvious distaste forced out the word—"*relationship.* So what do you say we try to make the best of it?"

For a moment Sarah was too surprised to respond. This overture was the last thing she had anticipated, and she couldn't imagine what lay behind it.

"It'll get your mom off your back," Kyra continued hurriedly, as if she was afraid Sarah was going to hang up on her. "She keeps bugging you about getting involved in school activities. I bet this would make her happy."

"What do you care if my mother's happy?" Sarah asked suspiciously.

"I don't," Kyra said. "But you do. And you know as

well as I do that she's not going to find much happiness here."

There was a moment of silence as Sarah struggled unsuccessfully to come up with an appropriate retort. As much as she hated to admit it, Kyra was right. Rosemary, who was obviously a victim of middle-age insanity, had sacrificed the career and friends of a lifetime to follow her heart to a little town filled with narrow-minded bigots and take on the dubious role of a married man's "lady friend." Even if Ted did marry her, she would never be accepted here. The most she ever could hope for would be simply to be tolerated.

As that thought took form in her mind, Sarah found herself struck by a feeling of such abrupt and intense foreboding that it was as if a black void had opened directly in front of her. In that instant of dislocation, as she fought to maintain her equilibrium and keep from tumbling headfirst into the pit of darkness, a voice seemed to shout directly into her right ear.

"Guilty as charged!" it bellowed. *"Away to Gallows Hill!"*

"No!" Sarah heard herself whimper. *"I didn't really mean it!"*

"Poor little Betty," another voice said more gently. *"The child is too frightened to remember."*

Betty does remember, and she's sorry! She never should have done it!

For an instant the chasm gaped wider, and then the illusion was gone as if it had never been. With a gasp of relief, Sarah found herself safe again in the living room, where the only activity was on the television screen and the only voice was Kyra's, tinny and tiny at the other end of the phone line.

"You didn't mean *what*?" it was asking. "Does that mean you've changed your mind?"

"Yes," Sarah said. "I guess so. But for Rosemary's sake, not yours. I couldn't care less how 'cool' you think Eric Garrett is."

She replaced the receiver in slow motion and sat down on the sofa, feeling as if she had served a short stint in the Twilight Zone. Whatever had caused her to have such a bizarre hallucination? *Gallows Hill*, she thought, *what a horrible name!* Why did it seem so familiar, as did the name Betty? Had she read or heard about something like this on television?

"That's what I get for not eating," she told herself shakily. "Low blood sugar can make people dizzy and disoriented."

It was not until she was standing at the microwave, watching the plate of lasagna rotate behind the glass, that she fully realized what she had agreed to.

What have I let myself in for? she thought with dismay.

Like it or not, she had committed to playing a fortune-teller.

chapter
THREE

The carnival officially started at seven P.M. The gym doors opened to a flood of miniature clowns, pumpkin heads, and fairy princesses accompanied by their parents. The high-school crowd, most of whom considered themselves too cool to wear costumes, arrived slightly later in groups or as couples, plunking down their one-dollar admission fee at the door and glancing about admiringly at a room that could no longer be recognized as a gymnasium.

Sarah had been startled herself when she arrived a little after six to find that the members of the Carnival Committee had been able to alter the atmosphere of the room so completely. Streamers of orange and black crepe paper crisscrossed the ceiling; maliciously grinning jack-o'-lanterns lined the window ledges; and a bubbling cauldron filled with dry ice projected a churning cloud of steam. The bleachers had been disassembled and moved out to make room for a variety of booths ranging from games of chance to those selling homemade candy and bake-sale items. An area at one side of the room had

25

been roped off for a cakewalk, and on the other side a stuffed dummy dangling from a gallows marked the entrance to a plywood spook house.

The fortune-telling tent was positioned against the back wall, flanked on one side by a Pop a Balloon and Win a Prize game and on the other by a Kiss the Spider Lady booth. The tent was made of sheets, dyed black for the occasion, with a large, hand-lettered sign that challenged the faint-hearted, DARE TO ENTER AND LEARN YOUR FUTURE FROM THE INCREDIBLE MADAM ZOLTANNE!

When she stood at the entrance to the tent, Sarah could see Kyra on the far side of the gym, seated next to the Bite an Apple on a String booth. She was dressed as a ghost. The costume totally concealed her identity, and in her hands there was an unlit jack-o'-lantern.

Eric, outfitted as a circus ringmaster, seemed to be everywhere at once, checking on details and trouble-shooting last-minute problems. He paused to speak briefly to the ghost and then crossed the gym to Sarah.

"You look great!" he said in a low voice, glancing around quickly to make sure he wasn't overheard. "I can't see the earphones at all."

"Is Kyra miked yet?" Sarah asked him.

"The microphone's in the jack-o'-lantern." He reached over to make an adjustment in the angle of the sign. "You haven't told anybody about our gimmick, have you?"

"Who would I tell?"

"I thought maybe your mom or Mr. Thompson."

"I promised you I wouldn't," Sarah said stiffly.

"I like a girl who can keep a secret," Eric said approvingly. "You're going to be the hit of the evening."

Sarah was not nearly so optimistic. When the gym doors opened to admit the first rush of early arrivals, she stepped back into the tent and took her seat in a chair behind the small circular table that held her crystal ball. She adjusted her scarf and waited. Time went by, and nobody entered. The room beyond the tent flap was filled with voices and laughter, and she could hear loud popping sounds as people broke the balloons in the booth next door.

Finally, when she had just about accepted the fact that the evening was over for her before it had even started, the curtain parted and a girl with long blond hair stepped into the tent.

"Hey! You really do look like a Gypsy!" she exclaimed in surprise.

"I am Madam Zoltanne," Sarah told her, experiencing a rush of unexpected stage fright. She had seen the girl around campus, running with the jock crowd, and she knew she was one of the cheerleaders, but she didn't know her name.

The girl handed over her ticket and paused uncertainly.

"What do I do now?" she asked.

Sarah motioned her into the chair across from her. The girl sat down gingerly, as if expecting the bottom to fall through, while Sarah gazed down into the ball, trying to act as if she saw something fascinating in its depths. The earphones beneath her headgear remained stubbornly silent, and she was struck by a wave of panic. What if the radio wasn't working?

Then, to her relief, the earphones crackled into life, and Kyra's voice burst upon her eardrums.

"That's Cindy Morris. Her dad's the minister at Pine Crest Community Church. She's adopted, but nobody's supposed to know it. She bleaches her hair, and she used to wear braces. When she was little, she had a grubby old baby doll named Dorcas that she dragged around with her everywhere."

Sarah stared into the ball, trying to assimilate the shotgun torrent of splattered information. She decided to start with the basics.

"Your name," she said softly. "I see a round letter. It must be an *O*—no, it's half an *O*—the letter is *C*. Cindy is the name, isn't it? I can't quite see the last name, but it does seem to be a bit longer than the first name, and it seems to me that the two middle letters are the same."

"Morris," the blond girl said. "I'm not surprised you know that. Everybody knows the cheerleaders."

The statement was offered as a challenge, but Sarah ignored it.

"Morris," she repeated. "Yes, that's what it is—Morris. But there's something wrong with the letters. They keep shifting around. It's like they're not sure they belong there—as if there was a time when your name was something else."

"I don't know what you're talking about," the girl said nervously.

"Maybe I'm wrong. Things aren't always what they seem. If you did have another name, it was at a time when your smile looked different and your hair was darker."

"What do you mean, 'darker'?" Cindy demanded in a defensive voice. "I'm a natural blonde."

"Like I said, things aren't always what they seem," Sarah said. Her eyes remained glued to the crystal sphere. "The person I see in the glass is not the same as the person who is sitting across from me. In the glass I see past the outer shell into the soul. What I see is an insecure child in need of a friend. No, wait—she *has* a friend—someone—something . . ." She leaned closer to the glass. "She is hugging someone and gaining comfort, but it's not a flesh-and-blood person. It's too soft and cuddly to be a person. It's a . . . doll!"

"So what else is new?" Cindy said. "All girls have dolls when they're little."

"Not like this one," said Sarah. "This doll has a distinct personality. She has an old-fashioned name. Her name . . ." She paused for effect and then said softly, "Her name is Dorcas."

There was a long pause.

Then Cindy exclaimed, "How did you know that?"

"I am Madam Zoltanne," Sarah said as if that explained everything. "Now the glass grows dim and the pictures fade. Peace be with you, and may the stars in the heavens watch over you."

The girl left the tent, and Sarah drew a deep breath. She couldn't believe it had gone so well! For once her mother had been right; all her experience in high-school theater was paying off.

Cindy's place was taken by a little girl in a Minnie Mouse costume.

"That's Amy Albritton." Kyra's voice spoke into Sarah's headphones. "I sometimes baby-sit her. She's in second grade and has an older sister named Jennifer. She's a *Sesame Street* freak and watches it every afternoon. She's afraid of the dark, so her folks gave her a Big Bird night-light."

Talking to Amy was easy, because the child had been so conditioned by television that nothing struck her as fantastic. Although Sarah mentioned her sister, Jennifer, by name and made a subtle reference to the night-light—

"A big yellow bird watches over you every night"—Amy didn't seem too impressed. What she did respond to was Sarah's improvised description of what her life would be like as an adult when she appeared on screens throughout the country as "a glamorous movie star."

Amy went rushing out of the tent, eager to share the news of her thrilling future with her mother. No sooner was she gone than a teenage girl took her place.

"This is cool!" she said. "Cindy's right, you do look like a Gypsy. What can you read about me in that magic ball?"

Even as the girl spoke, Kyra was filling Sarah in on her.

"Leanne Bush is Cindy Morris's best friend. She dates Bucky Greeves, the captain of the football team, but he's got a crush on one of the other cheerleaders."

It wasn't much to go on, but Sarah did her best.

"I see you with a boy—very strong physically—he's looking at you and smiling, and you're smiling back at him. But his eyes are gazing beyond you."

"That's my boyfriend, Bucky," Leanne said. "You say he's looking past me? What's he looking at?"

"I can't quite see," Sarah said. "She's standing in the shadows."

"It's Debbie!" Leanne exclaimed. "I just bet it's Debbie Rice! What does she look like? Does she have thirty-eight-D boobs?" She didn't pause long enough to get an answer. "It *is* Debbie, I *know* it is. I've suspected it all along, but Bucky keeps saying I'm being ridiculous. That two-timing slime ball! He's no better than any of those other jerks! How long has this been going on?"

"I can't see anything now," Sarah told her, a bit startled by the outburst. "The ball has been emptied of vi-

30

sions. Peace be with you, and may the stars in the heavens watch over you."

Leanne left the tent, visibly shaken, and from then on people arrived in a steady stream. No sooner did one leave the tent than another stepped in, and when the flap was pulled back, Sarah could see that there was a long line of prospective clients waiting their turns.

It was evident that people were busily spreading the word about the amazing Madam Zoltanne, because each client seemed to generate others. Bucky Greeves arrived with a chip on his shoulder, announcing that Leanne had sent him.

"She's pissed off at me," he said irritably. "What kind of bull did you feed her?"

"I tell each person what I see in the glass," Sarah informed him. "Nothing more or less." She realized to her amazement that she was actually enjoying herself. With only a few exceptions when she had to wing it because the costume concealed a wearer's identity, she received feed-in from Kyra about everyone who entered the tent. Although she was glad for the information, Sarah couldn't help wondering about someone who knew so much gossip, especially family secrets, such as the fact that Cindy Morris was adopted.

She took Bucky by surprise by revealing her knowledge that when he'd had chicken pox at age five, his mother had sent him to kindergarten anyway and he had infected the whole class; that he would have flunked first-year algebra if the coach hadn't pulled some strings to keep him on the football team; and that he was a heavy-duty pot smoker. She also let drop the name Debbie and watched his face turn crimson. He was immediately on his feet and out of the tent.

As Bucky exited, Kyra's voice said, "The one who's coming in now is our paperboy. His name's Charlie Gorman, but behind his back everybody calls him Lard Ass. He's sort of like the class clown. His mom is a bookkeeper or something, and his dad's a cripple. The guys on the football team found out the combination to his locker and last week they put a dead fish in it."

By this time the boy was in the tent, easing himself into the chair across from Sarah. He was definitely overweight, and his extra chins were nestled one on top of the other like towels in a linen closet. Still, there was something likable about his face, and Sarah immediately decided not to mention the fish.

"I hear you tell great fortunes," the boy said good-naturedly. "So, what do you see for me?"

Sarah lowered her eyes and stared into the ball.

"Your name starts with an *O*," she began, in repetition of the beginning of her fortune for Cindy Morris. "No—wait—it's only half an *O*."

"I'll save you the trouble," the boy said. "The name's Charlie. You may not have noticed, but I'm in your history class, two rows over and three seats back. What I'm interested in is what do you see in my future?"

Kyra's voice fed in through the earphones. "Tell him he'll be manager of a fish store."

What a horrid girl, Sarah thought, feeling a surge of sympathy for the boy across from her. This poor guy had enough problems without having people continue to make fun of him after the joke was over.

She decided to give him a good fortune, something pleasant to look forward to, even if they both knew it was only a game.

"I see you on a cruise ship headed for Hawaii," she

said. "You're dressed in a tux, and you're with a beautiful woman. It's obvious that you're very rich and successful. The orchestra's playing, and you and this lady are getting up to dance. You're—"

Something was wrong.

The globe on the table was no longer clear; it seemed to be filling with smoke that was twisting and turning within it, creating shadows that were superimposed upon shadows. In the midst of the smoke she saw the stocky figure of Charlie Gorman poised at the top of a flight of steps. A foot came out from behind him and snagged his ankle, and with a shout of surprise he pitched forward.

chapter
FOUR

Sarah stared into the ball in silence, unable to believe what she was seeing. The figure in the glass waved his arms wildly in a desperate attempt to regain balance, clutching frantically at the air. Then he plunged down the steps with his arms thrust straight out in front of him and disappeared into the thick coils of smoke at the bottom of the globe.

"What is it?" Charlie asked. "Is all that good stuff too exciting for you to handle?"

"It's—it's—" Sarah raised her eyes and focused upon the round, pleasant face across from her. In the dimly lit tent it was hard to see Charlie in detail, but she felt certain that he was the same person as the figure in the smoke.

Or had she seen anything at all? Perhaps her eyes had been playing tricks on her, as they had when she'd seen that flash of yellow in her mother's bedroom mirror. After all, she had been staring into the globe all night, straining to appear as if she were focusing on something.

She glanced back down at the ball. It was as clear as

window glass. No smoke, no visions. Obviously her imagination had been working overtime, but the experience had been scary.

"I'm sorry," she told Charlie shakily. "I don't see anything."

"You mean I don't have a future?"

"Of course you have a future. I just don't see it, that's all. You know it's all just a game, and I'm getting tired. It's been a long evening."

"The carnival folds at eleven," Charlie said sympathetically. "It's almost that now, but you've still got a long line waiting. Do you want me to tell them you're closing up shop?"

"Would you, please?" Sarah said gratefully. "I don't think I can handle any more of this. I'm sorry, and I'll see that you get your money back."

"Don't worry about that. It was worth it to hear about the cruise ship. Maybe next time we do this you can get me onto the dance floor."

The heavyset boy got up from the chair and shoved the tent flap aside, and Sarah leaned back in her chair and let her eyes fall closed. She was exhausted, and she suddenly realized she was getting a headache. She could hear a chorus of voices reacting with disappointment to Charlie's announcement that the booth was shutting down.

"That's not fair!" a girl's voice complained. "I've been waiting in line fifteen minutes! Everybody says that Gypsy girl's amazing!"

"I want her to tell me if Jennifer's going to let me get lucky tonight," a male voice bellowed with a macho laugh, and a girl with no laughter in her voice said, "You are so *crude*, Danny."

"What's going on?" Kyra's voice came crackling through the earphones. "Why is the crowd breaking up? It isn't time to close down yet."

"Don't you try to tell me what to do," Sarah said out loud, although of course there was no way Kyra could hear her.

She pulled off the earphones so that she would no longer have to be subjected to Kyra's voice, although she had been hearing it for so long now that it still echoed in her head. Then she took off the Gypsy outfit and dumped everything into a tote bag that she had stashed beneath the table. Under the costume she had been wearing jeans and a T-shirt, and when she lifted the back flap of the tent and stepped out into the gym, nobody gave her a second glance.

Charlie had been right, the crowds were definitely thinning out. The elementary-school children had pretty much disappeared, but a number of high-school students were still horsing around, shoving each other's heads into the Dunk for Apples tank and tossing battered-looking pumpkins at the dummy on the gallows. She caught a glimpse of her mother and Ted standing by the door with Ted's nine-year-old son, Brian.

Sarah hoped this didn't mean that Ted's kids were coming home with them. The last thing she wanted to do was join the group, but there was no way to avoid it, since they were obviously waiting for her.

Her mother saw her approaching and gave her a big smile.

"From the comments I've heard, the fortune-telling booth was a huge success! I kept hearing people raving about the fabulous Madam Zoltanne!"

"Great job, Gypsy lady!" Eric called to her, striding

toward them across the gym, with Kyra, as usual, bobbing along beside him as though attached by an unseen thread.

"Boy, what a night!" he exclaimed enthusiastically as he came up to her. "We haven't had a chance to tally up yet, but from the looks of the cashbox, we're going to have one great prom."

"We had good promotion," Kyra said.

"And some red-hot drawing cards. Like I predicted, your booth was the hit of the evening, Sarah. I wanted to get my own fortune told, but the line was too long. How would you feel about giving me a private reading?"

"You know it was a hoax," Sarah said.

"But a fun sort of hoax. Everybody loved it."

"Can we go to your house and eat brownies?" Brian asked Rosemary, who now directed her smile at him and said, "We certainly can, honey."

"Do you want to come back to Rosemary's?" Ted asked his daughter, wording the question for Eric's sake in such a way as to mask the fact that he was living there as well.

"No, I've got other plans," Kyra said. "A bunch of the kids are going to the Halloween Special midnight movie. Eric will take me home afterward."

She put a slight emphasis on the word *home*, another subtlety that Sarah caught but was in this case far from opposed to. It was nice to know that Kyra recognized that her "home" was with her mother.

"Want to join us, Sarah?" Eric asked as if it were the most natural thing in the world.

"I don't know . . . ," Sarah said, taken by surprise. She had no desire to do anything social with Kyra, but it was Eric, not Kyra, who was inviting her, and this was the first time anyone in Pine Crest had asked her to do anything. She was on the verge of accepting, when she suddenly remembered the sad state of her finances. She had two dollar bills and a small amount of change in her jeans pocket.

"Our treat, for both of you girls," her mother said quickly.

"Right!" Ted agreed, groping in his pocket for his wallet.

"I don't need money," Kyra said. "You gave me my allowance yesterday."

"Sarah . . . ?"

"I'm fine too," Sarah said stiffly. "I'm just tired, but thanks anyway, Eric. It was nice of you to ask me."

They left the gym together and split up in the parking lot. Sarah got into the backseat of Ted's Ford with Brian. The boy, who had the same red, curly hair as his father and sister, was a nonstop talker and jabbered all the way home. Unlike Kyra, he seemed to have latched on to Rosemary as a second mother.

At the house Brian headed straight for the kitchen, followed by Rosemary, who set out the brownies and then opened the freezer to get out ice cream.

"Our own Halloween party," she said happily. "What flavor does everybody want, chocolate or strawberry? I should have gotten orange sherbet to go with the decor, but I just didn't think about it."

"Chocolate for me," Ted said. "And Brian will want both. Sarah?"

"Nothing, thanks," Sarah said.

"We've still got the spice cake . . . ," Rosemary began.

"I'm not hungry."

Leaving the little family of three at the kitchen table, Sarah went down the hall to her bedroom. She flicked on the overhead light, closed the door, and dumped the tote bag onto the second bed. Then she stuck a tape into the cassette player to listen to while she changed into her nightshirt.

New Age instrumentals usually had a soothing effect on her, as if they were resting her soul and giving light to her spirit, but tonight was different—she couldn't concentrate on the music. Her eyes kept being drawn to the tote bag. She finally sat down on the bed, reached into the bag, and took out the crystal ball. The muted light of the tent had lent it a magical quality, but in the bright glare of the overhead fixture it was only a paperweight, round and smooth with the bottom leveled off so that it could stand flat on a desk. She wondered how her mother had produced it so quickly. The moment Sarah had announced her intention to participate in the carnival, Rosemary had gone straight out to the garage and reappeared with the ball, saying, "Here! Doesn't this make a perfect crystal ball? It almost seems like that's what it was made for."

There was a rap at the bedroom door.

"Sarah?" her mother called softly. "You're not asleep already, are you?"

"No," Sarah said. "Come on in."

Rosemary opened the door and came into the room, with Yowler at her heels. She was carrying a bowl of strawberry ice cream.

"I thought maybe you'd changed your mind about being hungry. I got the strawberry especially for you."

"That does look good," Sarah said, ashamed of her earlier pettiness. Her mother's efforts to please her were becoming embarrassing.

"I wish you'd gone out with Kyra and her friends," Rosemary said, setting the bowl on the bedside table next to the crystal ball. "It could have been the start of a social life. Ted says Eric Garrett is a real key to meeting people. He comes from a prominent family; his father is a lawyer, and his great-grandfather, Samuel Garrett, was founder of this town. Besides that, Ted says he's very popular and is involved in everything."

"I couldn't afford to go out tonight," Sarah said.

"But Ted offered to pay!"

"I won't take Ted's money," Sarah said. "Besides, I'm tired and didn't feel like it." She gestured toward the crystal ball. "Changing the subject, where did that thing come from?"

"Out of one of the crates in the garage. It was right on top."

"I don't remember ever seeing it before."

"I didn't have it out when we lived in the apartment."

"Then where—?"

"It belonged to your father's mother," Rosemary told her. "She died right after your father and I became engaged. The paperweight was one of the few things your dad brought back with him after the funeral. After his death it got packed away in a box with the other stuff from his desk. I forgot all about it until we were packing to move here and discovered the box on a shelf at the back of the coat closet."

"I don't think I've ever even seen a picture of that grandmother," Sarah said.

"You look quite a bit like her," said Rosemary. "You

40

have the same coloring. She was Hungarian and very exotic-looking. Of course your father had black hair and dark eyes too. I always felt sort of pallid and washed out next to him."

"Rosie?" Ted called from the hall. "Brian's ready for bed. Do you want to come tell him good night?"

"I'll be right there," Rosemary called back. "Good night, Sarah, honey. You'd better get started on that ice cream. It's already melting."

Sarah dutifully ate the ice cream, letting Yowler lick the bowl clean afterward, and then, overcome by fatigue, crawled into bed, almost too tired to make the effort to turn off the light. She fell asleep immediately, but despite her exhaustion it was a restless, dream-haunted sleep. When she awoke in the morning, she could not remember much about the dreams, but was conscious of a rancid mental aftertaste, as if her head had been filled with an unpleasant substance.

The house was so quiet that she knew nobody else was up yet. The thought occurred to her that this would be a good chance to peruse the classifieds in the Sunday paper. There was no getting around it, she had to find a job; she couldn't go through a whole year here without any spending money, and she was determined not to lower herself to accepting a handout from Ted.

She got dressed and let herself out of the house into a crisp autumn morning that should, under normal circumstances, have been invigorating. Instead she was struck by the same odd sense of foreboding she had experienced when she and Rosemary had crossed the peak of Garrett Hill and gazed for the first time at the tiny town of Pine Crest nestled in a hollow at its base. "What a sweet little town!" Rosemary had exclaimed in delight, and Sarah had been forced to agree that the neat little tree-lined streets and pitched-roof houses had the charm of a picture postcard designed by Grandma Moses. There had been no valid reason for the words that had leaped into her mind, as sudden and stark as if somebody else were dictating them: *This is a frightening place, and I don't want to live here.*

Now she shivered and wrapped her arms around herself, wishing she had put on a jacket, as she glanced around the yard for the paper. As if on cue, an elderly-looking station wagon pulled up in front of the house and a middle-aged woman with short brown hair turned awkwardly in the driver's seat to dump a newspaper out the window. It didn't make it as far as the yard, and landed with a slapping sound on the sidewalk.

Sarah moved to retrieve it, and the woman called, "Sorry about that! I'll never make it to the majors!"

"Don't worry about it," Sarah responded. The woman's round, pleasant face looked familiar, and she knew immediately who she must be. "Are you Charlie's mother?"

"Yes, I'm Lola Gorman," the woman said. "I'm filling in for Charlie today, but he's going to have to find himself a substitute pretty quickly, because I work on the weekdays and don't have time for this. The doctor said it will be at least three months before he can throw papers again."

"What happened?" Sarah asked in surprise. "I just saw him last night!"

"He was leaving the carnival and tripped coming down the steps in front of the school," Mrs. Gorman told her. "In trying to break his fall, he broke his right wrist."

chapter
FIVE

At school on Monday Sarah found herself the object of more attention than she had received since her arrival at Pine Crest. Instead of the sensation that she was invisible, she felt as if there were a neon sign on her forehead that caused all eyes automatically to turn in her direction. It wasn't exactly as if she were engulfed in friendliness. Students whose fortunes she had told greeted her cautiously (except for Bucky Greeves, who averted his eyes and charged past her as if she were Typhoid Mary). But at least there was an obvious awareness of her existence, which was more than she had encountered before. And, better than that, when she stopped at her locker to do a book exchange midway through the morning, she found Eric Garrett there waiting for her as if he had memorized her schedule.

"Guess where I spent the last half hour?" he said with a grin. "In the principal's office, getting chewed out by Mr. Prue. He said the carnival was only supposed to have games and things, and he's now been informed that it was a hotbed of spiritualism."

"A hotbed of spiritualism!" Sarah repeated incredulously. "What in the world is he talking about?"

"Not to worry, I was able to sweet-talk him out of it," Eric said easily, seeming to relish this sort of challenge. "I told him you and I had miscommunicated and that each of us thought the other had gotten permission. Then he switched gears and started in on the witch's cauldron, how it was a symbol of the occult and had no place at a school function. I told him he'd gotten it wrong and that the kettle with the dry ice in it was meant to represent Jack Frost's paint pot. That calmed him down."

"What's wrong with him?" Sarah exclaimed. "Is he some sort of fanatic?"

"It seems that some kid's parents complained to Reverend Morris, and he got on Prue's case after church service yesterday," Eric said. "Like I said, not to worry, I was able to handle it. You did a dynamite job. The whole school's talking about it. You should have heard all the comments when we went out afterward. Everybody was raving about the incredible Madam Zoltanne."

"I forgot to give you back your radio," Sarah said. "I'll bring it to school tomorrow along with the Gypsy costume."

"That's not too great an idea," Eric said. "Somebody might see it and realize how we faked things."

"What difference would that make now?" Sarah asked, bewildered by his reaction.

"I'd like to keep everybody mystified for a while," Eric said. "At least until I've had a chance to talk to you about something. If you don't have anything planned for right after school, I'll give you a ride home and pick up the radio at your house."

"That would be fine," Sarah said with a rush of pleasure.

"I'll meet you in the parking lot. Do you know which car is mine?"

"I think so," Sarah said, almost laughing aloud at the question. She couldn't count the occasions on which she had watched wistfully as that bright red Charger shot off down the street with its cargo of laughing young people, headed for the Burger Barn, or the bowling alley, or the rec hall at the church, or whatever the scene of that afternoon's action. More often than not, the person in the seat beside Eric had been Kyra Thompson.

In history class she glanced about for Charlie Gorman. He was exactly where he had said he would be, two rows over and three seats back from her own seat. When she caught his eye, he gave her a wry half smile and lifted his right arm high enough for her to see the cast that covered his wrist and a large part of his hand. There were holes for his fingers to come through, and he wiggled them at her, one at a time, as if they were finger puppets. The memory of the plunging figure she had seen in the glass came back to her with such force that it was almost frightening. The fact that Charlie had fallen later that same evening was a coincidence eerie enough to give her goose bumps.

She intended to ask him about it after class, but at the end of the period the teacher handed out instructions about a term paper that would be due at the end of November. Scanning the list of possible subjects, Sarah was surprised to see that one of them was printed in boldface.

On her way out of the room she paused at the teacher's desk to ask about it.

Mrs. Larkin seemed surprised by the question. "Boldface? Which subject is in boldface?"

"The Salem Witch Trials," Sarah said. "I guess it was just a printing error."

"It's certainly not in boldface on my copy," Mrs. Larkin said, squinting at the sheet on her desk. "Either you need your eyes checked, Sarah, or I do."

"On *my* copy it's—" Sarah began, but broke off the statement as her eyes went back to the printout in her hand. Nothing on it was printed in boldface. No item on the list of suggested topics stood out from the others. "I guess it's my eyes that have the problem," she said apologetically. "The topic just sort of jumped out at me. I could have sworn it was printed darker than the rest."

"Maybe it was the lighting," Mrs. Larkin suggested.

"Yes, I guess it must have been."

By now the rest of the students, Charlie included, had left the room, and she had lost her chance to ask him about his accident.

However, she did see him again at the end of the day, squatting by a floor-level locker, awkwardly trying to work the lock with one hand. It occurred to her that anyone standing over him could easily have learned the combination just by watching him. No wonder it had been so simple to plant a fish in his locker.

"Could you use some help?" Sarah asked, coming to stand next to him.

Charlie glanced up with a rueful smile. "Well, if it isn't the Gypsy lady! Thanks, but I've got to learn how to manage one-handed. It's going to be a while before I get rid of this hunk of plaster."

He gave the dial a final twist, and the metal loop popped open.

"There, I got it!" Charlie said with a note of triumph in his voice.

"I hear you fell on the steps the other night," Sarah said.

"I hold you responsible," Charlie said as he pulled the locker door open. "I got so pumped up by that business about the cruise ship that I thought I was diving into the ocean. It's the story of my life that there didn't happen to be water in it."

"How did you fall?" Sarah asked him.

"Like a ton of bricks."

"I mean, how did it happen?" Sarah prodded. "Did somebody trip you?"

Charlie turned to stare at her. "What makes you ask that?"

"I don't know. I mean, it seemed like a possibility—"

"Of course nobody tripped me," Charlie said quickly. "Why would anybody do that?" He turned back to the locker. "Actually I guess I do need some help with this. Do you think you could haul those library books out from under that heap of gym clothes?"

"Sure," Sarah said, dropping to her knees beside him. When she leaned into the locker, the stench of rotten fish almost bowled her over.

"I didn't get tripped," Charlie repeated, sounding almost defensive. "I stumbled over my two big feet. This isn't my lifetime to be coordinated. In my next incarnation I plan to be a graceful ballerina."

"Do you really believe in reincarnation?" Sarah asked him.

"It makes as much sense as anything," Charlie said. "Voltaire said, 'It's no more surprising to be born twice than to be born once.'"

"I never thought of it that way," Sarah said, surprised that the "class clown" would even know who Voltaire was. "It might be worth being born a second time to see you do a pirouette." She took out the books—and let out a groan at the sight of their titles.

"What's the matter?" Charlie asked her.

"They're all on the Salem witchcraft trials. Is that what you're going to do your report on?"

"I thought I would. It's more interesting than the other topics. I figured everybody else in the class would decide the same thing, so I hightailed it to the school library at lunchtime and grabbed up the only three books on the subject. Needless to say, our library is not exactly made for heavy research."

"Then that's it for me," Sarah said glumly. "I was also planning to do my paper on that subject."

"No problem," Charlie said. "You take one book home and read it, and I'll take the other two. Then we'll trade. Everybody else is out of luck."

He slammed the locker closed with his left hand and then attempted unsuccessfully to snap the lock back in place.

"Here, let me," Sarah said, reaching over and securing it. "Anything else I can do for you while I'm being useful?"

There was a long pause.

Then Charlie said tentatively, "How would you like to throw newspapers?"

"You mean, take over your paper route? I don't have a bicycle."

"You wouldn't need one," Charlie said. "Mom will let me use her car as long as I get it back so she can drive it to work. I can drive and point out the houses, but I can't throw. You can have full pay for the couple of months you'll be doing it. I just don't want to lose the route. If they hire a substitute, I'm afraid I won't get it back."

"That sounds good to me," Sarah said. "I need to earn some spending money, and there's nothing in the classifieds that looks even possible. When would you want me to start?"

"Tomorrow, if you can. Mom did the papers this morning, but she sure wasn't happy about it."

"What time?" Sarah asked.

"I'll pick you up at six-thirty, and we should be done in about an hour. It takes longer than that with a bike, but the car will speed things up."

"Do you know where I live?" Sarah asked him.

"Of course. You're on my route."

"Then I'll see you in the morning," Sarah said. "I'll be outside waiting."

She straightened up easily, while Charlie lumbered to his feet and thrust one of the three history books into her hand. "Want to start with this one? It's the thickest."

"One is as good as another," Sarah said. "Thanks. I'll see you early tomorrow."

She continued down the hall and out through the wide front door. She couldn't help noting that the cement steps that led down to the flagpole area were wide enough that it was hard to imagine anybody stumbling off one. Still, accidents did happen, and Charlie seemed the type who might be prone to clumsiness.

Eric was waiting for her in the Charger. The afternoon sunlight streaming in through the window glinted off his hair and made him appear to be wearing a golden helmet.

"So there you are! I was starting to worry that I was being stood up." He leaned across and opened the door on the passenger's side so that she could slide in next to him.

"I stopped to give Charlie Gorman a hand with his locker," Sarah explained. "He fell Saturday night and broke his wrist."

"Yeah, I heard about that. Poor old Gorman, stuff like that is always happening to him."

Eric started the engine, and Sarah glanced surreptitiously around, in the hope of spotting Kyra enviously watching them, but the lot had pretty well cleared out, and neither Kyra nor the group she ran with was in evidence.

"I have an idea I want to run past you," Eric said as they pulled out into the street. "That performance on Saturday was a blockbuster. It blew people away. Everybody at school today was talking about it. The ones who didn't get their fortunes told feel like they were cheated."

"I got worn out," Sarah said apologetically. "Besides, it was almost over."

"Don't get me wrong, I'm not complaining. You were obviously terrific. But there were plenty of kids still in line when you closed up shop. The more they hear about how mysterious it was—how right on target you were about everything you told people—the worse they feel about not having gotten in to see you. I've even had people asking me if you're a junior, which would mean you'd be around to do it again next year."

"So, what are you getting at?" Sarah asked him.

"Private readings," Eric said.

"A fortune-telling business? You can't be serious!"

"I think it could be a profitable venture," Eric said. "Not only would we get the kids who didn't get a chance at it Saturday, I think we'd get a lot of repeats. The ones who did get their fortunes told have had time to think about it now and wish they had asked you more questions. They want another shot at it."

"I can just imagine how that would go over with Mr. Prue!"

"This wouldn't have anything to do with the school," Eric told her. "We'd do it out of school hours at some other place. And we'd swear all our clients to secrecy. Mr. Prue will never get wind that we're doing it."

"You keep saying 'we,' " said Sarah. "What part would you play?"

"I'd take care of the business end of things, do the promotion, take in the money, sort of act as your manager. That way you could keep yourself aloof from the nitty-gritty. The mysterious Madam Zoltanne shouldn't have to deal with the grunge work."

"And Kyra?" Sarah asked. "Is she going to be out in front hiding in a bush with the radio? Because if that's what the plan is, forget it. It was bad enough having to work with her at the carnival."

"Nothing like that," Eric assured her. "We won't need to use the radio. We'll have appointments set up in advance so that I can get all the information from Kyra ahead of time. And since she'll know who's going to be there, she'll be able to do in-depth research and dig up some really hot stuff."

"Won't people catch on to how we're doing it?"

"Maybe so, maybe not," Eric said. "That doesn't really matter. Nobody takes this seriously. They'll just be there for the fun of it. They'll be paying for entertainment, like going to the movies."

By now they had pulled up in front of the house on Windsor Street. Eric set the gearshift in park but left the engine idling. He turned sideways to look at Sarah, and she was struck all over again by the charismatic warmth of his personality and the mischievous twinkle in the depths of his hazel eyes.

"What do you say?" he asked. "Would you like to be partners?"

"I can't believe that you're actually suggesting this!"

"If you don't need the money . . ."

"It's not that I couldn't use the money. It's just that the concept's so crazy!" And then, to her own astonishment, she heard herself say, "I'll think about it."

"Don't take too long, or we'll lose the opportunity," Eric said. "We need to strike while the iron is hot. People are all revved up from the carnival right now, but the excitement is going to die down if we don't keep it building. You can't go back to just being 'that new girl from California.' We've got to capitalize on the mystique you established."

"I told you, I'll think about it," Sarah said. She opened the door and got out. "Thanks for the ride. I'll be out in a minute with your radio."

She hurried across the yard and into the house. As usual she heard sounds of activity from the kitchen, and this time the house was permeated by the smell of spaghetti sauce.

Without stopping to speak to her mother, she went on down the hall to her room. The tote bag containing the costume and radio was still on Kyra's bed, where she had set it when she got home Saturday night. She extracted the walkie-talkie and the gaudy, sparkly costume. She didn't know what to think about Eric's proposal. The income from Charlie's paper route would only be temporary, and it would be nice to pile up a backlog of cash. She was tempted also by the thought of an association with Eric that would lead to their spending enough time together to have a chance to really get to know each other. At the same time, the idea of a fortune-telling business was so unorthodox that it was almost impossible to imagine.

She glanced across at the paperweight on her desk. The glass seemed cloudier than it had been when she had left for school that morning, as if it had lost its clarity during the course of the day.

With the radio still in her hands, she crossed to the desk and stared down into the murkiness of the globe. She knew, of course, that it had to be her imagination, but the shadows seemed to be shifting, as if there were actually motion in the depths of the ball. When she leaned in closer, she saw what appeared to be the figure of a woman bent into a contorted position as if in terrible pain.

That's ridiculous, Sarah told herself firmly. *It's all my imagination. If I keep this craziness up, I'm going to be a nutcase.*

Snatching the Gypsy costume out of the tote bag, she tossed it over her arm and set off down the hall with it and the radio. She was halfway out the front door when she heard a crash from the direction of the kitchen.

And then a long, shrill scream.

chapter
SIX

Her first impression upon racing into the kitchen was that the room was awash with blood. Thick and clotted, it spattered the white walls and cabinets, dripped down the side of the stove, and plastered the arms of her mother, who stood, bent double in agony, as the syrupy crimson liquid pooled at her feet.

An instant later Sarah took in the aluminum pot, which was on its side on the linoleum floor, and realized she was wrong. The "gore" that transformed the kitchen into what appeared to be a butcher shop was in reality spaghetti sauce, and Rosemary's arms were not draining themselves of her life liquids, they were sizzling in a molten substance that had adhered to her skin like rubber cement.

"Oh, God!" Sarah gasped. "Oh, Mommy!"

The childhood name flew out of her mouth as if she had spoken it only yesterday, instead of half a dozen years earlier when, following the example of her friends, she had started calling her mother by her first name.

"What's going on? Who screamed?" Eric seemed to appear out of nowhere and, as he took in the scene, crossed the kitchen in three long strides to grab Rosemary and spin her around so that she was facing the sink. As she moaned in pain, he turned on the tap and thrust her arms under the rush of cold water.

"Get ice," he ordered Sarah as he adjusted the spigot so that the water gushed out full blast.

"Shouldn't it be butter?" Sarah stammered, groping numbly for the refrigerator-door handle. "I think I read somewhere that if you put butter on burns—"

"I said *ice!*" Eric barked. "And get it fast! Her flesh is still cooking!"

Without further argument Sarah grabbed for the handle of the freezer, jerked it open, and yanked out the ice trays.

"Hurry!" Eric commanded. "First ice and then some dish towels to wrap it in!"

Moving as if set on automatic pilot, Sarah followed his instructions, smashing the trays against the counter to loosen the cubes and snatching the dish towels from their rack to the left of the sink. Quickly and efficiently Eric fashioned ice packs and applied them to Rosemary's arms.

Choking back sobs of relief, Rosemary collapsed against the counter.

"That's so much better!" she gasped. "It's like getting a shot of painkiller! I've never had anything hurt so much in my life!"

In all the turmoil the sound of Ted's car in the driveway had gone unnoticed. Sarah was startled to find him suddenly in the midst of them, white-faced with horror as he took in the scene of chaos.

"What happened?" he demanded. "Who's been injured?"

"That's not blood," Eric told him. "It's tomato sauce. Mrs. Zoltanne's been scalded."

"It's my own stupid fault," said Rosemary, fighting back tears. "I was taking the sauce off the stove, and I didn't use pot holders. I lost my grip, and the pot slid out of my hands."

"How bad—?"

"To me they look like second-degree burns," said Eric. "I think you'd better get her to Urgent Care."

"I'm going with you," Sarah said as Ted placed a protective arm around Rosemary and began to steer her across the kitchen toward the entrance hall.

"There's no need for that," Ted said. "There's nothing you can do. You'll be much more useful if you stay here and clean up this mess."

"But Rosemary's hurt!" Sarah protested. "I want to be with her!"

"I'll be all right, honey," her mother assured her as she leaned against Ted's arm and allowed him to guide her. "Please, don't argue, just do what Ted says. And Eric, I don't know where you came from, but I'm very glad you were here."

Sarah followed them into the living room and stood at the window watching helplessly as Ted and her mother got into Ted's car and he backed it out of the driveway and turned right to head south toward town. Long after the car was out of sight, she continued to stand there, gripping the windowsill and struggling for control.

"Are you okay?" Eric asked, coming to stand beside her.

"Not really," Sarah said. "I'm not very good in emergencies."

"You did fine," Eric said.

"No, I didn't. I panicked. Poor Rosemary—it was so terrible. . . ."

"It could have been a whole lot worse," Eric said gently. "The truth is your mom got off lucky. What if all that boiling stuff had splashed up into her face?"

"How did you know what to do?"

"I'm an Eagle Scout," Eric said. "That was my dad's idea; he thought it would look good on my college application. Not that it's any of my business, but does Mr. Thompson always come charging in here like that without knocking? I mean, the guy acted almost as if he lives here."

"He does live here," Sarah said, not bothering to lie.

"I thought Kyra told me he has an apartment over on Barn Street."

"That's just to keep up appearances," Sarah said bitterly. "I can count on one hand the number of nights he's spent there. That man is a total hypocrite and he's also a control freak. He calls the tunes, and my mother and I are supposed to dance to them."

"*Tell* me about 'control freaks,' " Eric said shortly.

"You've had experience?"

"Like all of my life," Eric said. "My dad and Mr. Thompson came out of the same mold, except that Kyra's dad went to teachers' college and mine went to law school." He paused and then said, "You know, maybe you shouldn't get involved in the fortune-telling. It could be risky for you."

"What do you mean?" Sarah asked him.

"If Mr. Thompson found out about it, there would be hell to pay, especially after Mr. Prue's reaction to your carnival booth. As scared as you already are of Mr. Thompson—"

"I'm not scared of him," Sarah interrupted defensively. "What makes you think I'm scared of him?"

"You sounded like you were. I mean, didn't you say that you and your mom do everything he tells you?"

"I'm not a bit afraid of him, I just detest him," Sarah said. "Just because Rosemary has decided to let Ted Thompson take charge of her life doesn't mean he's going to control mine. I can make my own decisions about how I earn spending money."

"Does that mean you'll do it?" Eric asked her.

"Yes, I'll do it," Sarah said. "So, tell me the details. How will we work it?"

"Well, first there's the question of finding a location," Eric said. "Where does your mom keep her mop? We can talk things over while I help you clean up the kitchen."

Kyra Thompson answered the phone on the first ring. The voice was the one she had been hoping to hear.

"So, how did it go?" she asked eagerly.

"It couldn't have gone better," Eric told her. "Are you where you can talk?"

"I'm on the kitchen extension. Mom's in the living room watching TV, and Brian's at a friend's house. So, tell me. What happened?"

"At first I thought she was going to say no," Eric said. "Then, while I was sitting out front waiting for her to come out with my radio, her mom had an accident in the kitchen. I came to the rescue like one of those medics on television. From then on I had her eating out of my hand."

"What happened to Rosemary? Not that I care, I'm just curious."

"She took a bath in a pot of boiling spaghetti sauce."

"How bad is it?" Kyra asked. "Is she going to need skin grafts?"

"I don't know, but it's certain that she would have if I hadn't been there. Sarah freaked out, and the Zoltanne woman was just standing there cooking in the stuff. I rinsed her off and packed her with ice. Then your dad arrived and whisked her off to Urgent Care. I helped Sarah clean up the kitchen—what a job that was!—and by the time we were done, she was acting as if I was Sir Lancelot and champing at the bit to get our little business going."

"I'm surprised," Kyra said. "I really didn't think you could talk her into it."

" 'O ye of little faith,' to quote from last week's sermon by our esteemed Reverend Morris. My barrister father has bestowed upon me a double-tipped tongue."

"You'd think I'd have learned that by this time," Kyra said. "Still, you never cease to amaze me. When will we hold the first session?"

"As soon as possible," Eric said. "We don't want to lose the momentum. And guess where we're going to have it? In your father's apartment!"

"You're *what!*" Kyra exclaimed. "Now, wait a minute, Eric! That's going too far! If Dad ever found out—"

"He's not going to find out," Eric said. "According to Sarah, he spends all his time at their place. She likes the idea of putting one over on your father. She's going to sneak the apartment key off his key chain and have it

59

duplicated. Then she'll put the original back. He'll never even miss it."

"But what if he happens to go over to the apartment while you're there? He doesn't go there often, but you can never tell."

"There'll be no chance of that if he's spending the evening with you," Eric said. "You get to pick and choose when you want to be with him, so pick the nights we're going to be using the apartment."

"It makes me nervous," Kyra said.

"It shouldn't," Eric told her. "Even if we do get caught, you won't get the blame for it. Nobody even knows you were part of the fortune-telling scheme at the carnival, and they're certainly not going to guess you're involved with this."

"Why is this so important to you?" Kyra asked him. "It's not like you need the money. Your dad gives you anything you want."

"Not this," Eric said. "Only you can give me this."

"If you get caught—"

"I'll talk my way out of it like I always do. That's half of the fun. Come on, Carrot Top, be a sweetheart. I need you for the info."

"All right," Kyra said with a sigh. "But please, be careful. Make sure everything in the apartment is put back just like it was. Don't start taking risks just to test Dad and see if you get caught."

"Would I do that?"

"Yes, you might. What I'm telling you is *Don't*. No matter what you say, if Sarah gets caught, she's not going to take it alone. She'll make the most of a bad thing by dragging me down with her."

She placed the receiver back on the hook and went into the living room, where her mother was seated in her father's recliner. The wineglass in her hand was filled to the brim, although Kyra recalled it as having been almost empty at the end of dinner. Obviously it had been re-filled from the decanter on the coffee table.

"Was that your father?" Sheila Thompson asked immediately.

"No," Kyra told her. "It was Eric. He just wanted to chat." She paused and then, pained by the disappointment on her mother's face, offered her a consolation gift. "Guess what happened today to Rosemary Zoltanne? She dumped red-hot tomato sauce all over herself."

"Can't that woman cook?" Sheila responded contemptuously.

"Obviously not if she can't hang on to a cook pot."

"Was she injured badly?"

"It was bad enough so that Dad had to take her to Urgent Care."

"I know I should say 'Poor thing!' or something of that sort," Sheila said. "It's the Christian thing to be sorry when people get hurt, and you know how important it is to me to live by Christian values. But I'm only human. It's impossible to feel sorry for a woman who takes advantage of an argument between husband and wife to deliberately break up a happy family."

"I know," Kyra said. She sat down on the arm of the recliner and slipped her arm around her mother's shoulders. "Hang in there, Mom, we're not beaten yet. Dad will come back. He always has before."

"But this time it's different," her mother said. "This time there's that woman!"

"She won't last," Kyra said reassuringly. "This is his home, and we're his family. He's not going to leave us."

"What does he see in her? Is she pretty?"

"Not as pretty as you are."

"Does she have a career?"

"She did, but she doesn't now. Nobody here will hire a woman like that."

"Your father wants a homemaker. That's terribly important to him; he wants to find everything perfect when he comes home from work. He didn't object to my working part-time at the church, but when I told him I wanted to apply for that job as a legal secretary in Bridleville—"

"Rosemary is a lousy homemaker," Kyra said quickly in an effort to quell the recitation before the tears came. "She serves weird food—like artichokes."

"Do you think your father still loves me?" her mother asked in a little-girl voice filled with pleading.

"Of course," Kyra said with certainty. "If Rosemary Zoltanne hadn't jumped into the picture, he'd be here right now. This isn't going to last, Mom, I promise."

"You're such a comfort," her mother said, reaching up to cover Kyra's hand with her own. She paused and then asked, "How did Eric learn about the tomato sauce? He doesn't go over there, does he? He hasn't made a friend of that girl?"

"Of course not," Kyra said. "I guess he just heard it somewhere."

In bed that night, too stressed out to sleep, Sarah opened the library book Charlie had given her. If she hadn't known otherwise, she would have thought she was reading fiction:

In Salem Village, Massachusetts, in 1692, nine-year-old Betty Parris, the daughter of the town minister, and her eleven-year-old cousin, Abigail, would sit in the kitchen of the Parris rectory and listen to Tituba, a slave from the Spanish West Indies, tell stories about magic. Although Tituba had converted to Christianity, she still had charms for everything. She even taught the children how to see their future husbands by breaking an egg into a glass of water and finding pictures in the swirls.

Fun was a scarce commodity in this tiny Puritan community, where lives were devoted to work and religious observance. Dancing and games were forbidden, toys were regarded as time-wasters, and little girls weren't even permitted to have dolls.

When word began to circulate about the entertainment taking place in the kitchen at the rectory, Betty and Abigail were joined by a group of older girls. The leader of this group was a twelve-year-old girl named Ann Putnam.

In Salem Village, anything involving magic was considered evil, and the older girls began to worry that they would be found out. Since Betty was the youngest and inclined to be a chatterbox, they threatened her with terrible punishment if she told what they were doing. Betty, who was an impressionable child, became too nervous to eat and started having nightmares and screaming in her sleep. Her father grew concerned and took her to a doctor, who, finding nothing physically wrong with her, determined that her problems must be caused by witchcraft.

When the older girls heard this, they became more frightened than ever that Betty would talk and that they would be blamed for her condition. Then Ann Putnam got the idea that if she claimed to be bewitched also, she might be able to escape punishment. Timing her performance to take place in the minister's presence, she screamed and hurled herself to the floor as if struck down by evil forces. The other girls caught on and entered into the drama, shouting that they saw hideous figures and were being pinched by invisible hands.

What a horrid bunch of children, Sarah thought, laying the book aside. I can't believe anyone could take all their crazy talk seriously.

But no matter how silly the story was, she was grateful to have something to think about other than the terrible scene that had occurred in her own kitchen.

chapter
SEVEN

Eric inserted the key into the lock of the ground-floor apartment, opened the door, and groped around in the darkness in search of a switch. After a moment he found it, and the interior of the room was flooded with overhead light. He set down his backpack and Sarah's tape player and went around quickly pulling down window shades.

"We don't want the neighbors reporting that they saw lights," he said.

"So this is his apartment." Sarah placed the paperweight on an end table and glanced about her with reluctant curiosity. The living room was exactly as she would have pictured it. As colorless and unimaginative as Ted Thompson himself, it was carpeted in beige and furnished with the routine sofa, armchairs, coffee table, and end tables, and a set of empty bookshelves.

"It looks like the places he's rented before," Eric commented. "Typical no-frills digs for a guy paying child support. Is he chipping in on your mom's rent, or is she carrying it herself?"

"I think they're splitting it," Sarah said. "But my mother's share comes out of her savings, since she hasn't found a job yet. What do you mean, it's like the other places he's rented? Have he and Kyra's mother been separated before?"

"A couple of times," Eric said. "It's sort of like a power play. She doesn't stand up to him often, but if she does, he puts her in her place by packing up and walking out. Then he gets his own place for a while until he starts missing the comforts of home and decides to give her another chance. They make up, and everything's rosy until it happens again."

"So you think he'll go back to her?" Sarah asked hopefully.

"Maybe not this time, because he has your mother." Eric was clearly bored by the subject. "So, on with the show! Let's figure out the best place for you to set up shop."

Together they toured the apartment, which didn't take long, as it consisted only of the living room, kitchenette, and two small bedrooms, one of which contained nothing but a bureau, the two single beds having been transferred to Sarah's bedroom at the house on Windsor Street.

"Terrific!" Eric said. "We can use this one as the séance room. If there were beds, it would ruin the effect."

"We're not having a séance," Sarah protested. "That's what they call it when mediums call up spirits of the dead. All I'm going to pretend to do is tell fortunes."

" 'The Crystal Room,' then," Eric said lightly. "I like that, don't you? That sounds like a room in the White House. Why don't you go get changed, and I'll set things up."

He made a quick trip back to the living room to retrieve the portable tape player and the backpack, out of which he extracted a K Mart sack, which he handed to Sarah. When she opened it, she was startled to find not the Gypsy costume she expected but a witch costume, with a black cape and peaked black hat.

"What's this?" she exclaimed. "I thought I was going to wear the same outfit I wore at the carnival!"

"I couldn't get it back from the Drama Club prop room without explaining why I wanted it," Eric said. "What I ended up doing was hitting the discount counter at K Mart, but most of the Halloween costumes were already sold."

"I don't like it," Sarah objected. "The other costume was funky and fun, but this one's creepy."

"Sorry," Eric said. "It was either this or a skeleton, and I figured you wouldn't want your bones showing. Now, seriously, we've got to get a move on. Your first client, Jennifer Albritton, is due here at eight. Her boyfriend, Danny Adams, will be coming with her, but you'll read for each of them separately. The third will be Debbie Rice. I've scheduled them for fifteen-minute sessions separated by five-minute breaks. That way you'll have time to prep yourself between readings. Here's a packet of information, courtesy of our research lady."

He thrust a sheaf of papers into her hand and turned his attention to setting up the tape player.

Reluctantly Sarah went into the bathroom to change into the witch costume. It was immediately obvious that it was meant for somebody much smaller, but then, how many girls her age went trick-or-treating? She consoled herself with the thought that she would be seated behind a table and nobody would see that the skirt hit her just below the knees. The problem came with getting her arms into the sleeves, and the soreness of her right arm and shoulder muscles made her sharply aware of the fact that they had received an unaccustomed workout that morning. Throwing a paper from the passenger seat of a station wagon involved more of an athletic effort than she had anticipated.

Pulling the cloak around her shoulders (there was no way she was going to put on the ridiculous hat), she peered at herself in the mirror over the sink. The glass was smudged in places and spattered here and there with toothpaste, as if somebody had rinsed out his mouth and spat too hard. The sink had little hairs in it, the residue from an electric razor. This was Ted Thompson's mirror, his sink, his bathroom, his apartment. No matter how seldom he used the place, she had no business being here. Her mother would have a fit if she knew about it.

For a moment she experienced a twinge of guilt at the memory of Rosemary as she had seen her last, lying on the living-room couch, doped up on pain pills and loaded with antibiotics, while Ted and Kyra sat at a card table and played gin rummy. She ought to be home with her mother when she was feeling miserable, but what good would it do if she were? Rosemary had Ted to look after her and had actually seemed pleased when Sarah announced she was going out with Eric. In Rosemary's eyes, Eric Garrett could do no wrong, and both she and Ted were openly delighted that Sarah was finally starting to "get out and do things."

Well, it was too late to change her mind now, even if she wanted to, which she wasn't sure she did. After all, she rationalized, Ted Thompson had taken over *her* home, so what was so terrible about spending a few hours in *his*?

Turning away from the mirror, Sarah unfolded Kyra's notes. The top sheet was on Jennifer Albritton and contained the same sort of information that Kyra had provided for her at the carnival:

> *Jennifer's dad sells insurance; her mom works in a stationery store. She has a little sister named Amy—you did a reading on her at the carnival, she's the one with the Big Bird night-light. Jennifer pretends to be a vegetarian, but every couple of days she sneaks off and gets a burger. She and Danny have been hot and heavy since Christmas.*

Sarah left the bathroom and went back out into the bedroom. During the time she had been gone, Eric had managed to manufacture a mood of mystery. He had brought an end table in from the living room and covered it with a black cloth for the paperweight to rest on. The overhead light was now off, and the room was illuminated by a row of candles lined up on the bureau top.

He turned to give Sarah a critical inspection.

"How about more eye makeup?" he suggested.

"I don't want to look like Vampira," Sarah said.

"Nobody as pretty as you could look like Vampira," Eric said. "I just thought some dark shadows might make you a little more mystical-looking." He reached over to lay a gentle finger against the side of her face. "How about a smile?"

"Witches don't smile," Sarah said.

"Not for your clients—for *me*. I don't like to see you so

solemn, pretty witch lady. This isn't the Inquisition, we're here to have fun!"

The sound of the doorbell shattered the brief moment of intimacy.

"I guess that means there's no time for more makeup," Eric said. "I don't suppose it really matters with the candlelight. I've got the tape player plugged in over there in the corner. I'll give you a couple of minutes, and then I'll bring in your client."

He left, closing the door behind him and leaving Sarah alone in the candlelit bedroom.

Taking one of her collection of meditation tapes out of her purse, she slipped it into the player and turned the volume down almost as far as it would go. Then she took her seat at the table that held the crystal ball. The atmosphere here was quite different from that of the carnival. There she had felt linked to the activity going on outside the tent, and the shouts and laughter and conversation from the carnival participants had bled in through the loose-hanging curtains. Here there were no such distractions, only the soft background music of strings and woodwinds and the dubbed-in cry of a loon by a moonlit lake.

She peered into the globe, and in the flickering light of the candles it seemed less like a paperweight than it ever had. It seemed in fact to hold an iridescent light of its own.

She became aware of the sound of voices outside the bedroom door. Then the door swung open, and Eric ushered in the first client and closed the door again.

Jennifer Albritton stood staring at Sarah in apparent bewilderment, as if she didn't know what to make of her.

"Are you the same girl who did the readings at the

carnival?" she asked doubtfully. "I thought she was dressed like a Gypsy."

"I am the same person," Sarah told her, assuming her fortune-teller persona. "I am Madam Zoltanne. Sometimes I present one image and sometimes another. The outer shell is of no importance; the only thing meaningful is what appears in the glass."

She motioned to the chair across from her.

Jennifer giggled self-consciously as she sat down.

"I can't believe I'm doing this," she said. "My folks would kill me. You won't tell anybody, will you?"

"Everything that occurs in this room is sacred," Sarah assured her. "This is a place where secrets of the soul are revealed."

"This is totally far out!" Jennifer said. "Can you really do this? Do you really see things in that ball?"

Sarah stared into the globe in silence for a moment. Then she said quietly, "I see a young girl who looks up to you. You are her idol. She seems like a happy child, but at heart she is frightened. The darkness brings out the fear in her. A large yellow bird watches over her."

"That's my sister, Amy," Jennifer said. "She told Mom you said that at the carnival, and Mom didn't like it. She said yellow birds are supposed to be familiars of witches."

"I see duplicity," Sarah said quickly, changing the subject. "I see a two-sided coin, a two-sided soul within the person who sits before me. On one hand, she has made a commitment never to bring the flesh of an animal to her lips. Yet there are times—times when she cannot control herself, times when her carnal desires grow too powerful to resist. There are times of shame. . . ." She paused.

71

"It's not often," Jennifer said nervously. "Just once in a while. And then it's just chicken."

"That's not what the glass tells me," Sarah said, leaning closer to the paperweight. She wished that Eric could be there to enjoy her performance and to see that she was not always as serious as she appeared to be. There was a quicksilver sparkle about Eric that brought out the fun in her—a reckless, devil-may-care quality that reminded her of Jon, when he skimmed the top of a cresting wave on his surfboard. She was tempted to tell Jennifer, "I see something big and four-footed that says 'Moo,'" but decided that that might be overdoing it. Instead she said, "The beast that I see in the glass does not appear to have wings. But—quickly this image fades—too quickly for me to be certain."

Jennifer gave an audible gasp of relief.

"And now I see Christmas," Sarah said. "What a joyous holiday! Something wonderful happened at Christmastime. Your heart began singing."

"Yes!" Jennifer exclaimed. "That's when I started going out with Danny! We got together at the tree-trimming party at the church. He was just so cute! He came over to where I was standing and whispered in my ear, 'I wish you had a bow on you, 'cause then I could unwrap you.' Wasn't that an adorable way to come on to me!"

At which point Jennifer took full control of the session, rhapsodizing in detail about her romance with Danny Adams, who was scheduled to be Sarah's next client. So when Danny came in for his reading, she had learned so much about him from his girlfriend that she didn't have to use much that was in Kyra's notes.

For the third client, though, it was different, because she knew almost nothing about Debbie Rice except that she was regarded as a femme fatale and, according to Leanne Bush, had a 38-D bust. After Danny left the room, Sarah snatched at the fragment of time she had before Debbie entered to reverse the tape in the player and study the information Kyra had provided. It was evident that Kyra had no warm feelings for this girl, for her notes about her were vicious:

> *Debbie's a slut who comes on to every guy that breathes. She's even made a play for Eric. She's president of the Drama Club and also a cheerleader. The cheerleader bunch sticks together, so they act like they love her, but underneath they're all scared she's going to snag their boyfriends. Her older sister, Grace, is no better. She'll put out for anybody. If you want to send Debbie into orbit, mention her sister and a bodybuilder type named Buzz Tyson. Debbie had her eye on Buzz, and Grace snatched him away from her. Now Debbie's trying to get him back.*

Well, that's just great, Sarah thought as she reread the notes. There's nothing here I can use, it's all just cat scratch. She already knew that Debbie had a reputation for being a flirt, so she might get by with mentioning that, but the other material was malicious and unsupported slander.

When Debbie entered the room, Sarah regarded her tentatively, hoping that enough of her inner self would be exposed to supply the material for an impromptu reading, but there was little to work from. The girl who sat down across from her was dark-haired, big-busted, and sultry-looking, but there was nothing in that to give a clue about her background.

In desperation Sarah decided to take what she had learned from Leanne Bush at the carnival and work from that.

"I see you surrounded by adoring young men," she began, staring intently into the ball. "Other girls are jealous of your popularity. There is one in particular, a pretty blonde, who is very possessive. She is attached to a particular young man—I think he's a football player—but he looks past her, and his eyes are focused upon you."

"That's all?" Debbie asked in unconcealed disappointment. "For what this is costing, I expected something sensational. You haven't told me anything you couldn't have learned just from going to the same school with me. That's not what I came for."

"What did you come for?" Sarah asked, taken by surprise.

"To try you out," Debbie said. "I know you're a fake, but there are people around here who believe in this crap. They're even saying you can do it—I mean, *really* do it. I came here to prove you're a con. You're not able to tell people anything that you couldn't have picked up just from hanging out in the school rest room."

She was right, of course. But the challenging attitude irritated Sarah. After all, this was just a game, and everyone knew it; it wasn't as if she were actually supposed to perform magic. She found herself feeling sorry for Leanne Bush, who was threatened by the prospect of losing her beloved Bucky to such an obnoxious competitor.

"Wait," Sarah said impulsively. "I do see something else. Another woman steps into this picture. She's a little bit older than you are, but"—she took a stab at this one—"she looks a bit like you. I think you may be related. There are similarities, but she has something . . .

more to offer. There is one particular man, very muscular and handsome, who once was looking at you and now turns to look at her. The images are starting to fade now. . . . I cannot continue. . . ."

"You're making that up," Debbie said belligerently. "You don't see anything."

The crazy thing was, though, that suddenly Sarah *did* see something. She saw a man and a girl entwined in each other's arms. And she saw where they were. For a moment the shadows lifted and there was a very clear image of the girl, who did look a little like Debbie, and the man, who was turned away from her, so that Sarah could not get a good view of him, standing in a building that appeared to be a bus terminal. Both were wearing backpacks, and next to them stood two suitcases.

"I see your sister with a man named Buzz Tyson," Sarah said. "They're kissing, and I think they're at a bus station."

"What a witch you are!" Debbie exploded. She leaped to her feet, deliberately kicked over her chair, and stalked out of the room in a fury.

chapter
EIGHT

"Rumor has it that Madam Zoltanne's powers extend beyond Halloween," Charlie commented as Sarah scrambled into his station wagon on Monday morning. He was wearing a worn plaid jacket with patches at the elbows.

"How did you hear that?" Sarah asked in astonishment. She had not seen Charlie since Friday, as his mother had driven the paper route on the weekend.

"Word gets around," Charlie said as they drove south on Windsor. "I stopped by the Burger Barn on Saturday, and Danny Adams was there spouting his mouth off at the next table. He was telling his friends how his girlfriend wasn't with him because—in capital letters—SHE'S A VEGETARIAN. Wouldn't darken the door of a place that cooks dead animals. And then he jumped from there to how he and Jennifer got their fortunes told and how Jennifer got all uptight about the stuff you knew about her that you had no way of knowing. What's the deal? Have you opened your own business?"

"Well, sort of," Sarah said. "It's just for kicks. It was Eric's idea."

"It would be," Charlie said with a noticeable lack of enthusiasm.

"What's that supposed to mean?"

"Eric pulls stunts like that. He does it to spite his father, the head of the prestigious law firm of Garrote, Vulture, and Chapstick."

"They can't be called that!" Sarah exclaimed incredulously.

"I'm kidding," Charlie said. "Haven't you figured out by this time that I do a lot of that? Fat people have to, it's part of our image. The law firm is Garrett, Venture, and Chapman. Eric's been primed to step into it since he was in preschool. Why else would he run for every school office there is? It's tough to get into an Ivy League college if you're a graduate of Pine Crest High. You've got to stand out from the herd."

"That doesn't explain why he'd come up with an offbeat money-making scheme."

"That's the other side of him." Charlie slowed the car so that she could toss a paper onto a lawn. "You must have done a great job with your mumbo jumbo. Danny sounded pretty shook up."

"Almost everything I told Danny was what Jennifer leaked to me," Sarah said. "She probably doesn't realize how much she told me."

"Who else did you read for?" Charlie asked her.

"Debbie Rice," Sarah said, sending the paper sailing directly into a picket fence. "I'm sorry. That was a bad throw. Shall we stop so that I can go get it?"

"There's no time, they'll just have to live with it,"

Charlie said. And then, with more concern, "You did a reading for Debbie?"

"Yes," Sarah said. "She came in with a chip on her shoulder, and when she left, she called me a witch."

"Why would she say that?"

"Well, I was dressed like one, for one thing."

"You weren't dressed like a witch at the carnival."

"This was a different costume," Sarah told him. "Actually, though, I don't think it was the costume she was referring to. She meant it as an insult. I told her something she didn't want to hear."

Charlie slowed, and she pitched another paper. This throw was an improvement over the last one; the paper landed on the lawn.

"You could be causing some problems for yourself," Charlie said.

"How so?"

"Pine Crest is a conservative town."

"So Ted's told us," Sarah said. "It seems to me it's a hypocritical sort of conservatism."

"You got that right. Take that sweet bunch of cheerleaders, for instance, with the minister's daughter at their head. They're all of them in the church youth group and sing in the choir, and butter wouldn't melt in their mouths when they're around adults. But do you know where they hold their innocent little soft-drink-and-cookie get-togethers? At the party spot up on the hill where the football guys throw keggers after the games. From what I hear, a lot of stuff goes on up there that you'd think the school would catch on to. But Mr. Prue's a real expert at looking the other way."

"I hadn't heard about those, but I do know that Ted is

paying rent on an apartment he doesn't stay in just to keep up appearances," Sarah said. "I can't believe his friends and neighbors are that gullible. Everybody must know he's actually living at our house."

"They may not want to know that."

"What do you mean?"

"If they knew it, they'd have to do something about it," Charlie said. "For one thing, Mr. Thompson would lose his job. Nobody wants that. What they want is for him to repent and go back to his wife, which he usually does after a month or so. You're right when you say it's a hypocritical sort of conservatism. But it's in keeping with the standards of the town." He changed the subject abruptly. "You missed that last house."

"Are we going back for it?"

"Of course we're going back for it. Hanging a paper on the fence is one thing, missing a house is another."

"I wouldn't have missed it if we hadn't been talking so much," Sarah said irritably. "I don't see anything so terrible about telling a few fortunes. People know when they come that it's just entertainment."

"All I said was be careful," Charlie said. "You could be headed for trouble, especially if you tell fortunes wearing a witch costume. This town isn't just conservative, it's downright dangerous."

"I happen to think you're being paranoid."

"I've got reason to think I'm not, but okay, I'll keep my mouth shut."

They completed the route with little further conversation, and Charlie dropped her off at her house. As she got out of the car, Sarah was tempted to apologize for snapping at him—after all, he did seem to be sincerely concerned about her—but decided to let it go. It was bad enough to have Ted ordering her around without having Charlie start in on it too.

When she entered the kitchen, she found Rosemary and Ted seated at the kitchen table drinking coffee and working on a package of Sara Lee breakfast rolls.

"So, how's the papergirl?" Ted asked her in a friendly manner.

"Fine," Sarah said coolly, and then, addressing herself to her mother, "How's the arm this morning?"

"Much less painful," Rosemary told her. "I have an appointment to go to the doctor this afternoon to get the dressing changed."

"I'll take you," Sarah said.

"That won't be necessary," Rosemary said. "Ted's planning to do it. He's going to come home right after school to drive me."

"Which means I need to get there a little bit early to take care of some paperwork," Ted said, shoving back his chair and getting up from the table.

"I'd just as soon get there early too," Sarah said maliciously. "How about giving me a ride?" She knew what the answer would be, but she wanted to make him say it.

"I don't think that would be too wise," Ted responded a bit awkwardly. "It might start tongues wagging, if you know what I mean. There's no sense getting the gossip mills churning."

"Soon enough," Rosemary said lightly. "As soon as we're married."

"And when exactly is that going to happen?" Sarah asked. "Are you any nearer to getting a divorce, Ted?"

"It's in the works," Ted said curtly as he left the kitchen. A moment later they heard the front door close much harder than usual with a sound that Sarah might almost have termed a slam.

"You mustn't embarrass him like that, Sarah," Rosemary said. "He's doing his best to speed things up. It's Sheila who's making problems."

"What sort of problems?" Sarah asked. "Is it a matter of support money?"

"That and everything else she can think of," Rosemary said. "It's the dog-in-the-manger syndrome. She and Ted weren't happy together, but she can't stand the thought of losing him to somebody else."

"Eric says they've split up before," Sarah told her mother. "I don't understand how people can do that. I mean, I'd think you'd either want to be married or you wouldn't."

"It's not that simple," Rosemary said. "Ted and Sheila got married right out of high school, and Sheila worked two jobs to put him through college, so he's always felt indebted to her. That's why he didn't encourage her to go back to work full-time after the kids were school-age; he felt it was his turn to be the breadwinner. But somehow she couldn't accept that."

"What do you mean?" Sarah asked.

"They just grew in different directions. That can happen when people marry too young. Ted says Sheila suffers from depression, and she also has a drinking problem, which gets worse whenever she and Ted have an argument. Ted would have ended things long ago if it wasn't for the children. You know how devoted he is to Kyra and Brian. And of course their minister counsels against divorce."

"Since when does Ted go to church?" Sarah asked in surprise. Although she and Rosemary were not members of a particular denomination, they had made it a practice to attend services at a number of different churches in an effort to learn all they could about a variety of religions.

"He went to church when he lived with Sheila," Rosemary said. "They had Bible study on Wednesdays, and the kids are in the youth choir. The church seems to be the center of most social activity here."

"I've never heard Ted suggest our going," Sarah said.

"He feels it would be too awkward under the circumstances. Everybody belongs to the Pine Crest Community Church, so we'd be faced with all the people who are friends of Sheila's. After Ted and I are married and the dust has had a chance to settle . . ."

"You make it sound like it's the only church in Pine Crest," Sarah said.

"It is," Rosemary said. "There is only one church in Pine Crest."

"There's *nothing else*—not even a Catholic church or synagogue?"

"We're talking small town here, honey," Rosemary said. "There aren't any Jews in Pine Crest, and what few Catholics there are attend the Catholic church over in Bridleville."

"But that's thirty miles away! Pine Crest sounds like Salem Village in the seventeenth century!"

"There is only one church," Rosemary repeated. "It services the town. Don't ask me why, I don't know, that's just how it is. The Reverend Morris is the only minister in Pine Crest, and Sheila Thompson works part-time as church secretary. So, as you can imagine, Sheila has the support of the parishioners, and Ted doesn't want to alienate the community. That's why he wants Sheila to be the one to initiate divorce proceedings, and he's sure she will if he gives her some time to think it over. In the meantime he and I have a wonderful relationship. I only wish you'd accept that and try to be happy here."

"But, Rosemary, how can you say—?"

"Let's drop it, okay, Sarah?" Her mother cut her off in midsentence. "You'd better get a move on. The only reason we agreed to your doing this paper route was because you assured us it wouldn't make you late for school."

Where had her true mother gone? Sarah wondered miserably. The woman across the table from her, who used to be her best friend—an interesting, energetic woman with offbeat viewpoints, always eager to explore all angles of every situation—was sounding more and more like a female version of Ted Thompson every time she opened her mouth. And, to make it worse, Rosemary was right, it *was* hard to do the route and then make it to school on time, especially if she stopped long enough to eat breakfast. If she had known that Eric was going to suggest an easier way to earn money, she never would have committed to throwing papers for Charlie. But she had agreed to do it, and she couldn't let him down. It was bad enough to be an overweight paperboy called Lard Ass, but worse by far to be an overweight paperboy who had lost his paper route.

She grabbed up her tote bag, snatched the last of the cinnamon rolls out of the package, and went back out into the chilly November morning. Beneath her feet the sidewalk crackled with dead leaves, and above her, naked branches raked at the sky with sharp-nailed fingers. The houses that she was beginning to know from Charlie's paper route were the same cute picture-book structures that had presented such a welcoming image when she and Rosemary first gazed down at them from the top of

Garrett Hill. They did not look welcoming now; they looked closed off and secretive. Then again, perhaps it was only the fact that the panes now had frost on them that made the windows appear to be eyes with silver-plated cataracts, blinding the occupants to anything beyond their own walls.

Why was it, Sarah asked herself as she crunched her way toward school, that the streets of this town seemed strangely familiar, as if she had walked them before? Why did she feel so strongly that she had gazed up before through thin bare branches at a clear, cold sky that bore no resemblance to the cotton-clouded skies of southern California? And why, when she looked to the north, where the paved street ended and became a hard-packed dirt road that disappeared into the pines that carpeted the southern side of Garrett Hill, did it send a chill down her spine, as if she had seen it before in a childhood nightmare?

I hate this place, she thought with an involuntary shudder. *Rosemary can do what she likes, but as soon as I graduate, I'm out of here. I won't come back even for Christmas; I'll spend the holidays in California with Gillian's family. If Rosemary wants to see me, she can come there to visit me.*

She arrived at school just in time to make it to her locker before the final bell rang. She was crouched on the floor, in the process of reorganizing her books, when a pair of shoes rammed into her, almost knocking her over. She looked up to find Debbie Rice standing above her.

"Where did they go?" Debbie demanded in an icy voice.

"Where did who go?" Sarah asked her.

"Where did Grace and Buzz take off to? You knew they were at the bus terminal. So draw on those evil powers of yours to tell me where they went. Grace didn't say in her note."

"You mean they really were at a bus terminal?" Sarah asked. "I didn't know there was one in Pine Crest."

"There isn't, but there is in Bridleville. And don't act so surprised. You knew it! You saw it in the glass! Grace left a note saying she and Buzz were eloping, but she didn't say where they were going. So you tell me!"

"How do you expect me to know that?"

"The same way you knew the other stuff," Debbie said angrily. "Just look in your crystal ball. Where did they go for a honeymoon? Do you see them in a gambling hall in Las Vegas or under palm trees in Florida?"

"I told you I don't have any idea," Sarah said. "You told me yourself you don't believe in the readings. And you're right, it's all just a game. That crystal ball isn't magic, it's nothing but a paperweight."

"Then how did you know they were in a bus terminal?"

"I didn't know," Sarah repeated. "It's pure coincidence. I just popped out with that to be saying something. Get off my back, Debbie. If I knew, I'd tell you, but I don't."

The final bell rang as she slammed the locker door shut and clicked the lock back in place. When she got to her feet, she was relieved to find Debbie was gone—so relieved that she didn't even mind being late to class.

chapter
NINE

When Sarah went to bed that night, she picked up the book that Charlie had loaned her and continued reading at the place where she had left off, making notes as she read:

> The Reverend Parris invited ministers from neighboring parishes to gather in his home to pray for his daughter's release from the powers of the unknown witch who had enchanted her. While the prayer fest was in session, Betty Parris and her cousin, Abigail, raced into the room screaming that they were being chased by evil spirits. The other girls were summoned to explain this behavior, and convinced the ministers that they, too, were affected by demons.
>
> The Reverend Parris asked desperately, "Tell us, if you can, who has afflicted you thus?"
>
> At that the leader of the group, Ann Putnam, responded, "I am not afflicted. I am very well, Minister." Then, in immediate contradiction, she hurled herself to the floor, thrashing as though in agony and shrieking,

*"Please, Minister, tell them to leave me alone! I will
never put my name to the devil's book, no matter how
they hurt me!"*

*Stunned by this statement, Parris asked the other
girls if they knew who was directing demons to torment
poor Ann.*

*Betty, who had dozed off in a corner of the room,
stirred in her sleep and murmured as if from a dream,
"It's Tituba."*

*The other girls quickly agreed, and added, "Tituba is
not alone!" They then named two other women from
the village—Sarah Good and Sarah Osburn—and
identified them as witches also.*

Sarah fell asleep with the book in her hands, and soon
was swept into a dream so vivid that it surpassed everyday reality. However, this dream was not a replay of what
she had just read. Rather than a kitchen or a parlor, the
setting was a church—a church that seemed so familiar
that she could not believe she had not attended it many
times. It was filled with dark benches, and she was seated
in the front row. She knew there were girls on either side
of her, but she was smaller than they were and could not
see their faces. In a line in front of the girls stood three
frightened-looking women. Behind these women there
was a long table lined with solemn-faced men, and behind the table was the pulpit.

One of the men leaned forward and addressed himself
to Sarah.

"What do you have to say of these women?" he demanded.

"Nothing," Sarah whispered, averting her eyes.

"Don't look away when I ask you a question," the man

said irritably. "It makes it appear as if you have something to be ashamed of."

Sarah gazed up into eyes that were bulging with intensity, as if the pressure of all God's angels were shoving them outward so that they could more closely inspect evil. For one horrible moment she feared that they might burst from their sockets and come rolling across the table to land in her lap.

"Nothing," she said more loudly. "I have nothing to say about them."

But the instant the words left her lips, the girl on her left began shrieking, "Judge Hathorne, they are scratching me and biting me! I feel their teeth in my legs! Dear God, they are going to kill me!"

Then the rest of the girls on either side of Sarah began to scream.

The faces of the three women immediately became distorted, swirling and swimming like the images in the crystal paperweight, but just before they lost all resemblance to humans, they became recognizable as faces Sarah knew and recognized.

That was the point at which she herself began screaming, and she was screaming still when her mother shook her awake.

"Sarah, honey, wake up!" Rosemary was her mother again, the same dear mother who had held and rocked her as a child. "Everything's all right! It's just a bad dream."

"A dream?" Sarah murmured. A dream? But it had seemed so real! She reached for her mother's hand and grasped it tightly, like a lifeline leading back to sanity.

"Do you want me to stay here with you for a while?" Rosemary asked her.

"Rosie, no." Ted's voice came from behind her. "You don't spend the night sitting by the bed of a seventeen-year-old. Sarah's a little bit old to be afraid of the dark, don't you think?"

"Ted . . . if she's frightened—"

"I'm fine," Sarah said stiffly. "I'm certainly not afraid of the dark. It was just a nightmare based on something I was reading. Go on back to bed, Rosemary."

"You're sure you're all right?" her mother asked doubtfully.

"Totally sure," Sarah told her, aware of Ted still hovering disdainfully in the doorway. "And you can go back to bed too, Ted. I don't go plunging into your bedroom without an invitation, so I'll thank you not to come barging into mine."

The truth was, however, that she wasn't "totally sure" she was all right. After her mother's comforting presence was gone, the strands of the terrifying dream still held her ensnared. She thought about Betty Parris's dreams, the ones that had led to the behavior that had caused her to be diagnosed as bewitched. Sarah had a sense that she knew what the little girl's dreams had been, but refused to allow herself to dwell upon them. It was bad enough to have dreamed about the child who had experienced them.

Reluctant to fall back to sleep for fear she might dream again, she lay tensely awake until dawn, when she finally allowed herself to doze. Jolted awake minutes later by the blast of the alarm clock, she dragged on her clothes and stumbled out into the yard to wait for Charlie, so heavy-brained and groggy that she hardly knew what she was doing.

Charlie, when he arrived, seemed equally uncommunicative. After ten minutes of silence, broken only by occasional admonishments about where to throw papers, he switched on the radio. To Sarah's surprise, instead of the country music that most of the stations carried, she heard the soothing sounds of woodwinds accompanied by a harp.

"What station is that?" she asked him.

"It's a tape," Charlie said, reaching quickly for the eject button. "I was playing it on my way over. I'll get something else."

"No, leave it on," Sarah said. "That's my kind of music. The kids I ran with back home used to listen to it all the time. Where did you buy it, anyway? I wasn't aware of a store here that sells New Age music."

"Don't bother looking, because there isn't one," Charlie said. "All you're going to find is country, gospel, and Golden Oldies."

"But wouldn't you think there would be a market for something a little different? I mean, not everybody is drawn to exactly the same thing when it comes to entertainment."

"Bite your tongue," Charlie said. "We don't talk like that in Pine Crest. On the surface at least, 'entertainment' around here means church suppers and G-rated movies. The last time somebody here had the gall to open a store that sold anything controversial, it was burned down."

"You're kidding!" Sarah exclaimed. "What kind of store was it?"

"A little mom-and-pop bookstore that carried some books that people didn't approve of. Mind you, I'm not talking porno, I'm talking philosophy. Along with the Bibles and dictionaries and mysteries and romances, they carried books about things like reincarnation and feminism and Eastern religions. In the middle of the night a fire broke out in the store. The owner, who lived next door, woke up and saw the flames. He called the fire department, but they never showed up. Later they blamed the owner for not giving the right address. The owner tried to put out the flames on his own and caught fire himself."

"The poor man!" Sarah exclaimed. "I know now how painful burns are!"

"This was worse than with your mother," Charlie said. "Both his legs had to be amputated. The store was burned to the ground."

"That's a horrible story," Sarah said. "But how did they know it was arson? Couldn't it have been an accident, like maybe the wiring was defective or—"

"The owner had received some sketches of a burning cross in the mail," Charlie said. "At the time he didn't know what to make of them. Afterward he figured they'd been meant as a warning."

"Did he show the pictures to the police?"

"The police weren't interested. There's nothing illegal about mailing a picture."

"Where do you get your tapes if you can't buy them here?" Sarah asked.

"I get a catalog in the mail from a store in Arizona. They sell tapes and books and a lot of other interesting stuff. They even sell crystal balls that look like your paperweight."

"I suppose they advertise them as magic," Sarah said derisively.

"No, just as tools for people to use when they're meditating." He reached over and turned off the tape. "The music must be hypnotizing you. You missed two houses. We'll have to go around the block and hit them again."

They finished the route in the same silence in which they had begun it. As they pulled up in front of Sarah's house, Charlie said, "You can borrow the tape if you want it."

"Thanks, I'd like that," Sarah said. "I listen to mine so much that they're getting pretty old."

"Speaking of borrowing, how are you doing on that witch-hunt book?"

"I'm only partway through it," Sarah admitted. "I'm sorry to be so slow, but the subject gives me nightmares. Last night I woke up screaming, which didn't go over well with . . . other people in our house."

"I'm not reacting to it any too well myself," Charlie said. "I had a dream . . ." He let the sentence trail off.

Sarah was intrigued despite herself. "What kind of a dream?"

"I felt like there were weights on my chest and I was suffocating. What did you dream about?"

"Nothing as bad as that," Sarah said, although she wasn't sure that she meant it. Her nightmare had been about as bad as they come.

"Look, before you take off, there's something I need to say to you," Charlie said. "I'm probably going to make you mad like I did the other day, but I feel like I've got to say it anyway."

"Okay, say it," Sarah said.

"I hear you had a run-in with Debbie Rice."

"Word does get around fast!"

"Well, it took place out in the hall, so it wasn't exactly private. Sarah, you can't do that, not with Debbie."

"She's the one who started it."

"It doesn't matter who started it, you just can't do it. Not with one of the cheerleaders. That cheerleader bunch may bicker among themselves, but they're a tight-knit group; actually it's kind of unnatural, like they have a bond of some sort that goes back to another lifetime. And except for Eric Garrett, who's in a league of his own, the cheerleaders and the guys on the football team pretty well run the school. Cindy Morris—"

"She seems nice enough," Sarah broke in. "There's no reason for Cindy not to like me."

"She's the minister's daughter," Charlie said. "And Kyra's mom is church secretary. That's reason enough right there."

"Does that mean it's impossible for me to make a friend in Pine Crest? I'm only here because my mother lost her senses. If anybody's guilty of bewitchment, it's *Ted* who bewitched my mother!"

"I knew you were going to be mad."

"I'm not mad, I'm just . . . confused," Sarah said. "What did you mean about Eric being 'in a league of his own'?"

"I just meant he's not a jock, even though he hangs out with them," Charlie said. "His dad doesn't want him to 'waste his time' on athletics, so he's on the edge of that crowd, but not really one of them. He goes to their parties, and a lot of the girls have crushes on him, but he's got his own agenda. I wouldn't trust Eric Garrett as far as I could throw him—which wouldn't be far, even if I didn't have this cast on."

"So what exactly are you trying to tell me?" Sarah asked him.

"Don't do anything to irritate the cheerleaders, and cut out the fortune-telling."

"Anything else while you're handing out advice?"

"I think that's enough for one morning," Charlie said tonelessly.

It was a strange conversation, and Sarah tried her best not to dwell on it, but as the day went on, it kept clawing at the corners of her mind. Charlie's round face had been so earnest, and his voice had held a disturbing note of somberness that seemed totally out of character. At the end of the morning, when Eric intercepted her at her locker to tell her about the next week's appointments, she found that she had serious reservations.

"I've set you up with four clients for next Friday," he told her, obviously expecting her to be pleased.

"I don't know," Sarah said hesitantly. "There was one that didn't go so well last time. I'm starting to wonder if we shouldn't think twice about going on with this."

"What do you mean, one didn't go well?" Eric asked her. "As far as I know, they were terrific! Jennifer and Danny have talked you up to the point where kids are standing in line to make appointments. I'm thinking of raising the price so that we can all get rich on this."

"But Debbie was so angry—"

"That's the greatest promotion she could give you. She's spread it around to everybody that you can really see the future. What you told her about her sister running off with that bodybuilder—how did you ever come up with a gem like that?"

"There was information about Buzz Tyson in Kyra's Cliffs Notes," Sarah said, skirting the question. "How does she know so much about so many people?"

"She's a wannabe," Eric said. "Wannabes are like that."

"A 'wannabe'?" Sarah repeated blankly. "What sort of 'wannabe'?"

"A wanna-be-all-of-the-things-that-she-isn't," Eric said. "Cheerleader; star of the Drama Club; big-busted sex symbol; a beautiful, mysterious crystal-gazer who tells heart-stopping fortunes. Wannabes soak up information about the people they envy, and now Kyra's got the chance to spout it all out again. The poor kid takes after her mom, who's a wannabe career woman, though now, I guess, she's switched back to being a wannabe housewife."

"Everybody's a wannabe *something*," Sarah said.

"But some of us make things happen, while others just sit there. You and I are among the movers of mountains, and that, my lovely soothsayer, is why you can't back down on me for Friday. All your clients have paid in advance, and, like I said, you're going to have one more than last time. Actually I could have scheduled triple that number, but I didn't want to wear you out. Besides, if people can't get what they want immediately, it makes them a lot more eager, don't you agree?"

Without waiting for a response, he proceeded to take her books from her hands and walk her down the hall to her next class, just like Jon used to do at her school back in Ventura. Eric even walked like Jon, with super-long strides, so Sarah had to do a double-time trot to keep up with him. She was acutely conscious of the curious glances they were getting, glances that asked, "Is there something romantic going on here?" Despite her irritation that he had taken her agreement for granted, it was an ego trip to be escorted to class by the Sun God. And to be honest, she had to admit that her enjoyment was intensified by the sight of Kyra, who was trudging past them in the opposite direction, carrying her own books and glaring.

"So, what's with you and Sarah?" Kyra demanded as she scrambled into the passenger seat of Eric's car. "I saw you trotting down the hall like her pet puppy dog. The two of you looked like you were headed for the altar."

"Don't be silly," Eric said. "I'm just doing my job. The goose that lays the golden eggs has got to be pacified. I may even take her to a movie or something to keep her happy. Do you know how much we're going to be charging on Friday? Twenty-five dollars per reading!"

"You're kidding!" Kyra exclaimed.

"Nope. And nobody's complaining. Four people at twenty-five bucks per head is one hundred dollars. That's fifty for Sarah and twenty-five for each of us. That's not bad for an hour's not-so-hard labor."

"Why does Sarah get more than we do?" Kyra demanded.

"Because she won't do it for less, and it won't work without her. Don't bring it up to her, okay? It'll piss her off, and we don't want her bailing out on us. She's already starting to get edgy, and that's not good."

"I work as hard as she does," Kyra complained. "Digging up all that information isn't easy."

"You're a miracle girl, Carrot Top," Eric told her, ruffling her hair. "I loved that stuff you got on Debbie's sister and the bodybuilder. Where did you come up with that anyway?"

"I overheard it in the school rest room," Kyra said. "I was in one of the stalls, and Misty and Leanne were gossiping while they combed their hair."

"The more personal stuff like that you get, the better,"

Eric said. "Nobody will ever guess it's coming from you. It's common knowledge that you and Sarah can't stand each other. For this Friday night I want stuff that is really intimate, stuff that nobody knows, and I mean *nobody*. Think you can manage that?"

"I don't know," Kyra said doubtfully. "There's just so much you can get by eavesdropping on conversations. I don't want to look suspicious. And the really hot stuff doesn't get talked about in public."

"You're right," Eric said. "That's the stuff people talk about to shrinks. Or to doctors. Or to religious counselors, like Reverend Morris. He probably keeps notes on the people who come to him for counseling. Is there any chance those might be on file at the church?"

"Possibly," Kyra said uncomfortably. "But I wouldn't have access to it."

"Your mom is church secretary, right?"

"She doesn't sit in on counseling sessions. They're private."

"But I imagine she types up the notes?"

"Yes, probably," Kyra said.

"I bet your mom knows things about the residents of Pine Crest that would curl your hair. Who knows, between now and Friday, she might slug down a few glasses of *vino* and pop out with the answers to questions that were put to her just right by her loving daughter. It's always a possibility, don't you think?"

He leaned across the space between them and brushed his lips against hers.

"What do you say, babe?"

"Who knows?" Kyra said, trying to act nonchalant and hoping he couldn't hear the pounding of her heart. "I guess anything's possible."

97

chapter
TEN

Sarah knew she should get the book read so that she could swap with Charlie, but she couldn't seem to make herself do it. After all, she told herself, Thanksgiving was still two weeks away, and there were more immediate demands upon her time—other homework to do, letters to write to Gillian and Lindsay (she restrained herself, with effort, from writing to Jon, as she had already written to him twice since receiving his last postcard), and a good deal of housework and cooking, since Rosemary still had only limited use of her arm and Ted insisted that he didn't "have the touch for women's work." There was an algebra test to study for, and even some social activity, as Eric invited her to the movies Wednesday evening. She found it a bit disappointing that he took her straight home afterward instead of stopping at the Burger Barn, where the high-school crowd gathered after dates, but Eric was quick to veto that idea when she suggested it.

"You can't afford to get chummy with the same kids whose fortunes you're telling," he said. "We don't want Madam Zoltanne to lose her mystique."

On the plus side, he kissed her good night when he brought her home.

"Did anybody ever tell you that you're a knockout?" he murmured, holding her close for a moment, his cheek pressed to hers as if he didn't want to lose contact.

"Not for a while," Sarah answered softly. "I mean, never here in Pine Crest."

"Then let me be the first," Eric whispered, giving her a quick, tight squeeze before releasing her. "I bet you'll look like a movie star in a prom dress."

It wasn't exactly a promise of things to come, but it did suggest that there might be nice times in store for them.

Two nights later, when she informed Rosemary that Eric was again coming by to pick her up, Rosemary naturally assumed it was another conventional date like the one on Wednesday.

"Looks like you two are beginning to be a regular item," she said with a note of teasing in her voice. Ted had taken Kyra out to dinner at a restaurant, and Sarah and Rosemary had had a comfortable, no-frills meal together, which reminded Sarah of the ones they had shared in California.

"Don't get me wrong, I think it's great," Rosemary added quickly. "Eric seems like a lovely young man, and thank God he was here and knew what to do when I burned myself. I couldn't be happier that you're starting to have a real life here."

"I wish *you* had one," Sarah said, feeling suddenly guilty about deserting her mother for the evening.

"I could have gone with Ted and Kyra," Rosemary said. "Ted would have been glad to have me, but I thought it would be good for him to have some private time with his daughter. He was so happy when Kyra called to suggest they spend the evening together that it made me realize how terribly much he misses her."

"I didn't mean with Ted," Sarah said. "You see plenty of him. I was thinking about your doing things with friends like you did in California. Back there you were always so busy going to lectures and concerts and art shows, and here you don't have anything, not even a job."

"I went over to the school the other day and applied for work as a substitute," Rosemary said. "They said they'd call me if they need me, but they weren't too encouraging. They said they've already got a long list of substitutes."

"A substitute!" Sarah snorted. "The woman who received the Teacher of the Year award at one of the best high schools in California is groveling for work as a *substitute*? Give me a break!"

"There aren't many teaching jobs available in a town with one high school," Rosemary said. "Besides, Ted likes the idea of being married to a homemaker."

"Isn't that unrealistic for a man paying child support?"

"I'm not exactly a pauper," her mother said stiffly.

"You can't dip into the investments you made with the money from Dad's life insurance!" Sarah exclaimed. "You've always said you would only do that in an emergency!"

"I'm not going to do anything hasty," her mother assured her. "I do have other savings. And I'm sure I can find a part-time job doing something that will get me out of the house and bring in a little money. And as for friends, I'm sure that Ted and I will make plenty of friends as a couple—after we're married."

The sound of the doorbell saved Sarah from having to respond.

Ted's apartment was exactly as they had left it. The sofa cushions were plumped and undented, the kitchen appeared not to have been used, and when Sarah went into the bathroom to put on makeup, the hair shavings still decorated the sink and the towels on the racks were draped in the exact same way they had been the previous week.

"He hasn't been here once," she commented to Eric as she exited the bathroom to find him arranging candles on the bureau top. He had already moved in the end table and set up the paperweight.

"Where's your costume?" he asked in surprise. "I thought you were getting changed!"

"I decided not to wear it," Sarah said. "It was too small. Where's my cheat sheet? I'd better get busy cramming."

"Here," Eric said, digging a sheaf of papers out of his back pocket. "You'd do best to read them one at a time so that you won't get the stuff mixed up. You've got enough time between readings to prep yourself on each person."

Sarah began to skim the first paper.

"Cindy Morris? But I've already done her! I told her fortune at the carnival."

"I told you people would be coming back for more," Eric said. "She told me what she wants to ask you. She wants to know what happened to her doll, Dorcas. It disappeared one day and she could never find it. God knows why, but she's been brooding about it ever since."

"Kyra can't possibly know what happened to Cindy's old doll."

"Maybe not, but her mom does," Eric said. "Mrs. Thompson is good friends with Cindy's mother. She was there when poor Dorcas bit the dust, or maybe I should say 'went up in smoke.'"

"You mean Kyra is getting information from her *mother!*" Sarah exclaimed. "I just can't use that, Eric. I can't take information from *her!* It's bad enough to have Kyra involved, but her *mother* . . . ?"

"What difference does it make where the info comes from?" Eric asked reasonably. "You're giving your clients what they want, and nobody's getting hurt. And Mrs. Thompson is benefiting her own daughter. Kyra goes home with the same amount of money we do."

The doorbell chimed.

"That's Cindy now," Eric said. "It's time to get going, Madam Zoltanne. Do the same great job you did last week, and with four clients at ten bucks apiece, we'll each be over twelve bucks richer."

Before she could respond, he was gone from the room, and because there was no alternative, Sarah quickly skimmed the notes Kyra had made about Cindy Morris. Her stomach gave a lurch as she saw what they contained. Then she slipped them under the draped black cloth that shrouded the table and sat there stiffly waiting for Cindy to enter. After all, she told herself, it was only a doll. Most little girls lost their dolls in one way or another. She didn't have any of the dolls she had owned as a child, and if somebody had asked her what had happened to them, she couldn't have told them. It didn't matter enough to her even to wonder about it.

The door swung open, and Eric ushered Cindy in.

"Here I am again," the pretty blond girl said self-consciously as the door closed behind her and she took her seat at the table. She drew a deep breath and let it out slowly like a sigh. "I wouldn't be telling you this, except I think you know it already. After all, that's what you *do*— you look in that ball and *see* things."

"The crystal ball doesn't always give answers," Sarah said. "Sometimes the visions are cloudy."

"But all the things you told me last time were correct," Cindy said. "I didn't want to admit it, but you were right about everything. You said I once had another name, and I did. My parents adopted me when they were overseas doing missionary work, but nobody knows I'm adopted except their closest friends. And, like you implied, I do touch up my hair, and I did once wear braces. And I did have a doll named Dorcas." She paused, and when Sarah didn't respond, she asked, "What happened to her? What happened to Dorcas? I have to know what happened to Dorcas."

Sarah was swept by guilt at the intensity in Cindy's voice. There was nothing playful about this. It wasn't fun. She was hearing the deepest secrets straight out of the heart of a girl she barely knew, and she had no right to do that.

"I can't tell you," she said. "I don't know. This isn't what you think it is."

"I don't care what it is," Cindy said, her voice shaking. "I need to know what happened to Dorcas. I've worried about it for years. I'm afraid I left her somewhere, like out in the rain or in somebody's yard. I need to know what I did with her. She disappeared out of my life, and it was all my fault!"

Sarah shivered. This desperation was so unnatural that it gave her the creeps. Nobody should care this much about the fate of a plaything.

"Just look in the ball," Cindy pleaded. "Look and tell me what I did with her. I've felt so guilty for so long!"

There's no choice, Sarah thought. *I have to tell her what happened. But I'm never going to do this again, not ever!*

"You didn't do anything," she said, pretending to gaze into the ball but actually referring mentally to Kyra's notes. "Your mother burned the doll in a trash can in the alley behind your house."

"She *burned* her?" Cindy gasped in horror. "Why would she do that?"

"You'd had chicken pox, and you insisted on keeping the doll in the bed with you. The sores oozed pus all over her, and your mother was worried that she might be covered with germs. So she took her one night when you were sleeping, and went out and burned her. Mrs. Thompson was with her at the time. And she never told you because she knew how upset you'd be, but she expected you to forget all about the doll. She got you another one right away, a much prettier doll with a china face and real hair."

"I never forgot her," Cindy said in a strangled voice.

"Then maybe you should," Sarah said. "You're a senior in high school. How many years has it been? At least ten or twelve."

"The length of time doesn't matter when you lose somebody you love," Cindy whispered, struggling to hold back tears. She got up from her chair and stumbled blindly out of the room.

The next two readings, though not as bizarre as that first one, were far from lighthearted. Both clients were cheerleaders, and the information that Kyra had dredged up about them was totally inappropriate. Sarah's problem was that she had no other material to work with, as Kyra had not included anything benign. So, against her will, she found herself telling one girl that the crystal ball portrayed her as having a secret eating disorder and the other that her brother was not away at college as everyone believed, but was in reality at a drug rehab center. Both girls left looking stunned and very upset, and Sarah couldn't blame them.

Her final client, Misty Lamb, was also a cheerleader, and when Sarah saw what Kyra had written about her, she immediately decided there was no way she could give this reading.

"I'm sorry," she told Misty when she took her seat at the table. "I seem to have lost my abilities at the moment. That sometimes happens when I overuse my psychic powers. Ask Eric to refund your money."

"I don't want a refund," Misty said. "You've only done three readings tonight. I know because I've been waiting in the living room since eight. You did a lot more than that at the carnival. You've got to look in the glass and tell me what you see there." She paused. "You do see something. Don't pretend that you don't. You just don't want to tell me. Do you see a woman crying?"

"I told you, I've lost my abilities. . . ."

"Are there bruises on her arms?"

"I can't see her arms," Sarah said. "Misty, please—this isn't going to work."

"She pretends to people that she falls down," Misty said. "She says she's clumsy, but my mom isn't clumsy. What I came here to find out from you is, *is she ever going to leave him?*"

"The glass has grown dim," Sarah told her in a desperate effort to extricate herself from what was fast becoming an unbearable situation. "I saw a woman crying, but nothing beyond that. It is not for me to know what the future will bring for her."

"You knew Debbie's sister was going to elope with Buzz Tyson," Misty said. "That means you must have some sort of legitimate power. If you could see Grace Rice's future, why can't you see my mother's?"

"I didn't actually see that couple eloping," Sarah said honestly. "What I saw was two people in a bus station kissing each other. I didn't know who they were or what they were doing there."

"So tell me what you see about my parents," Misty demanded stubbornly. "Is my mother going to leave my father? She keeps promising me that she will, but she never does. Everybody thinks Dad is so wonderful and that he and Mom are so happy, and nobody knows the hell that goes on at home. If I ever told anybody, my dad would lose his job, and he'd take it out on Mom and probably kill her. Please, try to see what will happen. You did it for Debbie!"

Sarah sighed. She felt terribly sorry for this girl. Personally she couldn't imagine any woman staying with a man who abused her, but she had read about people who did. Sometimes, however, they did break away from their abusers, and she supposed there would be no harm in giving Misty a little reassurance that things might get better, if not immediately, then possibly in the future.

"All right," she said. "I'll try, but with no guarantees."

She leaned forward and stared intently into the ball.

"I do believe I see the woman you ask about," she said finally. "There are no bruises on this woman. She seems strong and self-confident and healthy. She is alone in her home. She is making a flower arrangement. There is no danger. Whatever once happened is behind her—she is beyond it now." At Misty's audible sigh of relief she continued, "Now the glass grows dim. . . ."

Except that it was not growing dim; instead it was glowing with a strange silvery light. And bathed in this light stood a woman like the one Sarah had just been describing, except that she *didn't* look "strong and self-confident and healthy." As Misty had said, her arms were covered with bruises and her face had the haunted look of an animal in a trap. She was making an arrangement of autumn leaves in a vase. And she did seem to be alone—except that suddenly she *wasn't*. A man strode into the room gesturing wildly, his face contorted with fury. The woman turned, startled, as if she had not been expecting him, and let the vase drop as she instinctively raised her arms to shield her face. The man's muscular arm rose high and started to descend—

"He's hitting her!" Sarah gasped, so shocked by the vision that the words came tumbling out at their own volition. "She was arranging branches in a vase, and without any warning, this man rushed in and started shouting at her! She dropped the vase, and there's water all over the floor. She's backing away from him—the floor is yellow linoleum—"

"That's our kitchen!" Misty exclaimed. "We have yellow linoleum in our kitchen! What's happening now?"

"I don't know," Sarah said. "I can't see."

"Why not?" Misty demanded frantically. "Why can't you see?"

"I don't know," Sarah said again. "It just disappeared on me. Look, Misty, don't let this upset you. I can't really do this. It's all just a scam, just a game. What I just described . . . I'm sure it was all in my mind. I knew your father was a wife beater because somebody told me."

"That can't be true!" Misty cried. "Nobody knows about it! I've never told a single soul, not even my best friends! And Mom wouldn't tell—not anybody—except maybe our minister. She's been getting counseling at the church, but Dad won't go with her. Dad is a counselor himself, so he feels like he's beyond all that. He thinks this is all Mom's fault for making him angry."

"I hope things get better," Sarah said. "I truly do, Misty. I'm sorry I said things that upset you. I was making them up."

"No, you weren't!" Misty cried. "I've got to get home to her!"

She jumped up in a state of near panic and rushed out of the room. Sarah could hear Eric's voice as he attempted to intercept her, Misty's own brief hysterical response, and the slam of the front door.

The crash of that door was like a period at the end of a sentence. Sarah snatched up the crystal ball and dropped it into her tote bag. Then she yanked the cord of her tape player out of the wall socket and carried the machine out into the living room.

"Never again!" she told Eric. "Tonight was the end of this!"

"What do you mean?" Eric asked in apparent surprise. "You're getting better and better. The bombshells you dropped tonight nearly blew the roof off."

"This is wrong," Sarah said impatiently. Why couldn't he see something so obvious? "Didn't you see the effect this had on Misty, not to mention what it did to poor Cindy? This started out as a game, but it isn't one now. Kyra's giving me terrible stuff to tell people, things that I have no business knowing. It's destructive! We're hurting people!"

"You can't quit now," Eric told her matter-of-factly. "I've got clients lined up for the next three Fridays. And Kyra's doing *her* part; she's already got information on the ones for next week. And I'm going to raise the prices. The way this is taking off, I bet we can get at least twenty-five bucks a head."

"Where are kids around here going to come up with money like that?" Sarah demanded.

"By skipping a few lunches or movies, or pilfering a couple of bills from the old man's wallet. If people want money, they can get it. And people *do* want this. We've proved it! Look at how successful it is! Come on, sweetheart, you and I are a team!"

He started to put his arm around her, but Sarah jerked away from him.

"Please, take me home," she said.

"Let's go for a drive and park someplace and talk this over. Like up on the hill maybe. Have you ever been up there at night?" Eric's tone became soft and persuasive. "The view in the moonlight is incredible. You look out over the town, and it's like a great big game board, with all the houses lined up as if they were chess pieces."

"I told you, it's over," Sarah said. "There's nothing to discuss. I should never have allowed you to talk me into this."

"You'll change your mind in the morning," Eric said with certainty.

"Don't bet on it," Sarah told him.

When she got home, she was unpleasantly surprised to be greeted by the sound of country music and to see a light shining through the crack at the bottom of her bedroom door. Her heart sank as she realized that Kyra had not just had dinner with her father but had come back with him to spend the night.

When she entered her room, she found Kyra seated on the second of the twin beds, painting her toenails. Her radio was installed on the dresser where Sarah's tape player usually sat and was tuned as usual to a country-western station.

"Your filthy cat has been sleeping on my bed again," Kyra said by way of greeting. "It got hairs all over my pillow." She paused. "So how did it go tonight?"

"Awful," Sarah said.

"How could it have been awful?" Kyra demanded. "All that juicy info I gave you should have blown them away."

"That was hurtful stuff," Sarah said. "Where on earth did you get it?"

"My mom knows a lot of sensational stuff about the parishioners," Kyra said. "She's church secretary. It goes with the territory."

"Your mother told you all that? What a vicious creature she must be!" For the first time ever, Sarah felt some sympathy for Ted, who had lived for almost twenty years with a woman whose mind was a garbage bin.

"It's not like she volunteered it," Kyra said defensively. "I had to pump her to get it. With no husband to talk to, Mom talks a lot to me. And of course she had no idea what we were going to do with it. Eric told me he wanted personal stuff that would stun people. It's going to piss him off if you refuse to use it."

"I already told him I'm done with this," Sarah said. "If the two of you want to keep doing this, you can find yourselves another soothsayer."

"Suits me," Kyra said with a shrug. "This wasn't my idea. I only went along with it because Eric asked me to. He does things like this to let off steam."

"What do you mean, 'does things like this'?" Sarah asked her.

"Eric does a lot of things people don't know about,"

110

Kyra said. "He's got this double image, like two sides of a coin. One side is what his father wants him to be—straight-arrow, A-student, class president, captain of the debate team—the kind of guy who gets accepted at Harvard. The other side is . . . the other side."

"Meaning what?" Sarah prodded.

"Once in a while he's got to do something to prove to himself that he's his own person," Kyra said. "So he lives on the edge a little. I understand it. I've always understood Eric. He and I are soul mates."

"You're welcome to each other," Sarah said. "I must have been out of my mind to have gotten involved with this. Back home I had a friend named Jon who was a little bit on the wild side, but he never made me feel manipulated. Eric Garrett is something else entirely."

She got into bed and, realizing that sleep was impossible until Kyra was ready to turn off the light and the music, picked up the library book and continued reading where she had left off:

Warrants were issued against Sarah Good, Sarah Osburn, and the slave Tituba, and on March 1, 1692, a trial was held at the meetinghouse. The magistrates sat at a table in front of the pulpit, with the audience facing them and the afflicted children in the front row. The prisoners stood in a line between the magistrates and the children.

All the prisoners firmly attested that they were not guilty. Sarah Good was examined first.

"Sarah Good, what evil spirit have you familiarity with?" Judge Hathorne asked her.

"None," she replied.

"Then why do you hurt these children?"

111

"I do not hurt them," Sarah Good insisted.

"Children, look here on Sarah Good and tell if she is the person who hurts you," the judge said.

Ann Putnam screamed and hurled herself to the floor, and the other girls followed suit, shouting that Sarah Good's spirit was scratching and biting them. Betty Parris looked confused and frightened, but when she realized that everyone was watching her expectantly, she started to scream also.

Sarah Osburn and Tituba were presented in the same manner, and the girls denounced them as well. All three women were found guilty of practicing witchcraft and sentenced to be hanged on Gallows Hill.

Sarah closed the book in a state of stunned bewilderment. That scene was the one she had dreamed about three nights earlier! The memory of the dream came surging back to her, and with a shudder of horror she recalled what had led her to scream.

The faces of the three women condemned to death had been those of Cindy Morris, Debbie Rice, and Misty Lamb.

chapter

ELEVEN

W hen Kyra got to school the following Monday, she was startled to find Cindy Morris waiting to intercept her out by the flagpole.

"Our group needs to talk with you privately, Kyra," Cindy said. "We've got a really bad problem, and we need your input."

Kyra was flattered and also a bit apprehensive. In keeping with her status as both a senior and the head cheerleader, Cindy devoted little of her time and attention to juniors. It had always been Kyra's secret dream to be a cheerleader, but she had never even had the nerve to try out for the squad. It wasn't enough to be cute and peppy and to know all the cheers; cheerleaders were also expected to be glamorous, long-legged, and sexy-looking. Kyra had long since accepted the fact that she had none of those attributes. Regrettably she, like Brian, bore a physical resemblance to their father rather than their mother.

"What's going on?" Kyra asked now, trying to sound as if exchanges like this one were everyday occurrences.

"We need to talk privately," Cindy repeated. "I've called

a meeting at noon in the girls' dressing room at the back of the gym. Nobody will be there during lunch hour, so we'll have it to ourselves."

"What's this all about—?" Kyra started to ask, but Cindy silenced her with a wave of her hand.

"We'll tell you about it then. This is highly confidential, so don't tell anybody about the meeting. And be sure to be there. It is very, *very* important."

Kyra's curiosity continued to build steadily throughout a seemingly endless morning that was extended even farther by the fact that the last class ran late because the teacher had waited too long to start handing back papers. Then two girls accosted her in the hall to ask her to have lunch at their table so that they could discuss plans for a cookie sale to raise money to purchase new hymnals for the church youth choir. By the time Kyra had disentangled herself from her friends with the excuse that she had to make a phone call, and had dashed down the hall and across the back courtyard to the gym, she was running ten minutes late for her meeting with the cheerleaders. She was brimming with fear that they might have grown impatient and left.

However, when she entered the dressing room, she found all seven members of the squad assembled there waiting for her. As her eyes flicked from one gorgeous, clear-complected face to another, and took in the long, shiny manes of straight, glossy hair—all of which, except for Debbie's, were an identical shade of blond—she was uncomfortably conscious of her own orange, flyaway curls; the masses of freckles on her nose; and worse still, the zit that had erupted overnight on her chin.

"So, what's up?" she asked nervously, resisting the urge to cover her chin with her hand.

"Shut the door," Cindy said. "We need privacy. It's about Sarah Zoltanne."

"About Sarah?" Kyra exclaimed in surprise. This was the last thing she had expected.

"We need to know some things about her," Cindy said. "And since you're her . . . her . . ." She left the sentence unfinished, obviously at a loss as to the appropriate term to use.

"I'm not her anything," Kyra said firmly. "My father's going out with her mother. That's my only connection with her."

"From what I hear, they're not just dating," Cindy said. "They live together, don't they?"

"My parents are separated, and Dad has his own apartment," Kyra said carefully. "Mrs. Zoltanne and Sarah are renting a house, and my father spends time there."

"And you spend time there with them," Leanne Bush said, making it a statement rather than a question.

"Yes, sometimes. But that doesn't mean that Sarah and I are friends."

"We know that," Cindy said. "It's obvious to everybody that you hate each other. And that's understandable. And it's why we feel that we can ask you some personal things about her. But before we do, we need your promise of confidentiality. Anything that you tell us and that we tell you stops right here. Because we think we may be on to something very serious."

"Like what?" Kyra asked.

"First, we need your promise that nothing that gets said here ever goes out of here."

"I promise," Kyra said immediately.

"Good. Then here's what we want to know. It's no secret that you sometimes sleep over at the Zoltanne

115

house, and that you and Sarah share a bedroom. So what does she do at night? I mean, after you're both in bed. Does she say her prayers?"

"I've never heard her do that," Kyra said.

"Not to anybody? Not to God or . . . to . . . anybody?"

"No," Kyra said. "At least she doesn't do it out loud." She thought that a rather odd question. Who else did people pray to if not to God?

"Is there anything strange that she does do at night when she's in bed?"

"Well . . ." Kyra searched her mind. "She does seem to have a lot of nightmares."

"What makes you think that?"

"She cries out in her sleep a lot. She moans and sobs and jabbers stuff. It's impossible to get a good night's sleep in that room, especially when my pillow's always covered with cat hair."

"Cat hair?" Leanne Bush repeated eagerly, pouncing on the comment. "You mean Sarah Zoltanne owns a cat? I don't suppose it happens to be black, does it?"

"Well, actually, yes," Kyra said. "That's why it's so nasty when it sheds on a pink bedspread."

"A *familiar*!" Leanne cried triumphantly. "Witches all have familiars, usually cats and birds!"

"She told my little sister, Amy, that she was sending a big bird to her bedroom at night," Jennifer Albritton said with a shudder. "Amy repeated that to Mom. Amy thought Sarah was talking about her night-light, but Mom's pretty sharp. She guessed right off that something wasn't right about Sarah. I mean, how could she know that Amy's a *Sesame Street* freak?"

"What else does she do in her room that seems unusual?" Cindy asked.

Kyra thought a moment and then said, "She plays weird music. There aren't any melodies, and the only vocals are chanting."

"I wonder what she does in that house when you *aren't* there," Jennifer said. "The cat and the bird thing is scary, especially if she's sending them in little children's windows. Maybe I ought to ask Danny and his friends to stake out the house just to see what kind of visitors come and go at night."

"You said Sarah talks in the night," Leanne said to Kyra. "Do you think she casts spells?"

"I don't know," Kyra said. "I can't understand her. But she and her mother sure put some sort of spell on my father. He's a whole different person from what he used to be. My mother is making herself sick, she's so upset about it."

"She's not making *herself* sick," Debbie Rice said with certainty. "What's more likely is that Sarah's put a curse on her."

"A curse?" Kyra repeated in bewilderment.

"Sarah's been doing something I don't think you know about," Cindy said. "We haven't any of us wanted to talk to you about it, because we know how she and her mother have destroyed your family, and we knew it would hurt you to have to discuss her with people you don't know well. But the time has come when we can't keep silent any longer. Sarah has been doing something evil, and I'm ashamed to say that all of us here have been her victims." She paused for effect. *"Sarah has been telling fortunes."*

"You mean at the carnival?" Kyra asked carefully.

117

"Well, of course she did it there, and almost all of us got our fortunes told. We thought it was just a game, like all the other booths. But the fortunes she told—they weren't your normal, carnival kind of fun thing. She told us things that she had no way of knowing. She even told me the name of the baby doll I had when I was little."

"That is pretty creepy," Kyra conceded, grateful that no one had pegged her as the source of the private information.

"But that's not the half of it," Cindy went on. "The thing is, later she started up a fortune-telling business, with Eric Garrett as her manager. When I asked Eric about it, he told me she talked him into it by letting him think the proceeds were going into the class treasury. A few members of our group who didn't get fortunes told at the carnival had heard about what she'd done there and— well, naturally they got curious. So, against their better judgment, they made appointments. Just for a lark. And of course for the good of the class. And where do you think she was doing this?"

"I can't imagine," Kyra said.

"It was at your dad's apartment on Barn Street! Mrs. Zoltanne probably agreed to keep him occupied so that Sarah could use his place. I don't know how Sarah got the key. Maybe she didn't need one. Maybe she has the ability to walk through locked doors. The fortunes she told at your dad's place were worse than the ones at the carnival. She actually put curses on people."

"What do you mean?" Kyra asked, startled.

"Do you want to begin?" Cindy asked, turning to Debbie.

"She told me she was going to force my sister to steal

118

my boyfriend," Debbie said. "You know how crazy I was about Buzz Tyson. I've never even looked at any other guy."

"Not even Bucky?" Leanne asked suspiciously.

"Never! Leanne, he's your boyfriend! I'd never even think about stealing a guy from a fellow cheerleader!"

Leanne remained silent and lifted an eyebrow.

"She said she was going to make Grace hit on Buzz," Debbie continued. "She was going to put a spell on them so that they'd go so wild about each other, they'd lose control and run off together. She looked in her crystal ball and saw them eloping! Of course I didn't believe her. I knew how crazy Buzz was about me, and he and Grace hardly knew each other. But when I got home that night, Grace wasn't there. And when I phoned Buzz's place, *he* wasn't there!

"Later that week Grace phoned us from Florida. She and Buzz were married by a justice of the peace—they didn't have the nerve to go to Reverend Morris—and they're living in a one-room walk-up with roaches. The only job Buzz could get was ushering in a movie theater, and Grace is a waitress at a diner. She says it was the mistake of her life and she doesn't know what got into her. Neither of them knows. It's just like some unseen force shoved them onto that bus." She paused, then said, "That unseen force was Sarah Zoltanne!"

"But how could she—?" Kyra began.

"It wasn't just them. Just wait till you hear what she did to Misty's mother!"

"I got my fortune told last Friday," Misty said. "The only reason I went was because I'd heard so much about her that I wanted to see for myself. She looked in the ball

119

and told me that my mother was alone in a kitchen with a yellow linoleum floor. How could she know the color of our kitchen floor?"

"I don't know," Kyra said in honest confusion. That was not part of the information she had given Sarah. She herself had never been in the Lamb home, and Misty seldom, if ever, invited people over.

"She said she saw my mother arranging leaves in a vase," Misty went on. "And then my mother dropped the vase, and it broke. There was water all over the floor, and Mom slipped in it and fell. When I heard that, I ran out of there and drove home like a bat out of hell. I raced into the house, and there was Mom, on the kitchen floor, just like Sarah said she'd be. She'd hit her head on the edge of the sink when she fell. I dialed nine-one-one and they sent an ambulance. If I hadn't gotten there in time, she probably would have died!"

"Your dad wasn't there?" Jennifer asked her.

"No, of course not," Misty said. "If my father had been there, he'd have taken her to the hospital himself."

"What made her drop the vase?"

"I don't know. She just did. Don't *you* ever drop things? I mean, *everybody* drops things."

"It had to have been Sarah," Debbie said. "There was nobody in that kitchen except your mother and the evil spirit of that witch girl. What do you know about her, Kyra? They never come to church. Are she and her mother members of some cult in California?"

"Your guess is as good as mine," Kyra said. "After hearing all this, I'm not going to sleep over at that house anymore. If my dad wants to see me, he can visit me at home."

"We don't want somebody like this in Pine Crest,"

Debbie said. "Cindy, why don't you tell your father about it? Maybe he could perform an exorcism or something."

"I can't do that," Cindy said. "He'd want to know how I knew, and I'd have to confess that I had my fortune told. My dad would be so furious, he'd disown me. A minister's daughter doesn't go to a fortune-teller."

"What about sending him an anonymous note?" Jennifer suggested. "We could give him the address and time of Sarah's next reading, and he could walk in on her and discover for himself what she's doing."

"That won't work," Kyra said. "She's quitting the business." The minute the words were out, she longed to snatch them back. She was not supposed to know that Sarah was telling fortunes.

To her great relief, her slip went unnoticed.

"Why?" Leanne asked her. "It seemed to be going great guns."

"I'm not sure why. I think . . ." Kyra groped for an answer. "I think Eric fired her."

"He fired her!" Jennifer exclaimed. "I thought he was going out with her! Danny and I saw the two of them at the movies, and he had his arm around her and everything."

"He took her out once, just to keep her happy," Kyra said. "As class president he kind of felt he owed her something because he thought she was earning all this money for the class." Kyra was in too deep, and she knew it, but there was no turning back, so she mentally crossed herself and plunged ahead with the story. "Then he found out she was actually pocketing it herself. I mean, every penny they brought in, she was sticking in her purse! When Eric discovered that, he totally blew her off. He told her he didn't want anything more to do with her."

"That's just as well," Misty said. "We wouldn't want any of our parents going over there. If we exposed the fortune-telling racket, our names would come out. And so would all the things she said about us in her readings. We wouldn't want that. I mean, some of that stuff was very personal."

"She said stuff about our families too," another girl said nervously. "She told me something about my brother, the one who's away at college, that nobody knows—absolutely *nobody*—and my parents would be sure to think that I was the one who told her. There would go my driving privileges for the rest of my life!"

"So it's up to us to get rid of her ourselves," Debbie said. "Maybe if we put a little pressure on her, she and her mother will get on their broomsticks and go back where they came from. What would you say to that, Kyra?"

"I can't think of anything that would make me happier," Kyra said. She smiled at her beautiful new friends, wishing she knew them well enough to hug them.

On Wednesday morning, when Sarah Zoltanne went to her locker at the end of third period to get her gym clothes, she found a sheet of paper stuck in the crack under the door. When she pulled it out and unfolded it, she found that it was a hand-drawn sketch of a gallows.

chapter
TWELVE

Sarah waited until after dinner to tell them about it, in order to spare Rosemary, who set great store by a pleasant dinner hour. It was as if it had been so long since she had had a man to please that she took what Sarah considered an inappropriate amount of delight in doing everything up perfectly, including a cloth and linen napkins and candles on the table.

Sarah thought this obsession might also have something to do with the fact that her mother had to be bored out of her mind with nothing to do all day but look at the walls. In the beginning, the move and unpacking, the painting of the rooms and arrangement of furniture, had kept her occupied. Now, however, these initial challenges were over. Her busy career and assortment of cultural interests lay behind her, along with all the friends she had left back in Ventura, and she had little to do all day except cook and count the hours until Ted and Sarah got home.

Even the "romantic" evenings appeared deadly to Sarah, as Ted seemed perfectly content to spend the after-dinner hours reading, grading student papers, or watching football on television.

So because of its importance to her mother, Sarah had honored the sanctity of the dinner hour. Now, however, as Ted settled himself on the sofa and reached for the TV section of the paper, she said, "Before you flick on the boob tube, Ted, I have something to show you."

She handed him the sketch of the gallows.

"What's this?" Ted asked, glancing at it without much interest.

"What does it look like to you?"

"A gallows."

"That's what it looks like to me too," Sarah said. "Do you know where I found it? Stuck in the crack of my locker."

"Who put it there?" Rosemary asked, coming to stand where she could look over Ted's shoulder.

"Who do you think?"

"You're getting into a very annoying habit of answering a question with a question, Sarah," Ted said. "If you know who put it there, say so. If you don't, say you don't. Which is it?"

"I don't know for a fact," Sarah admitted, "but I think it's ninety-nine to one that it's a message from your darling daughter that she and her mother wish Rosemary and I were dead."

"What a terrible thing to say!" her mother exclaimed.

"I'm saying it because it's true."

"Kyra is not that kind of person," Ted said, struggling to control his anger. "Admittedly she is having some problems adjusting to my relationship with Rosemary, but you at least should understand that. You've made it very clear that you would like to see our relationship fail so that you and your mother can regress to the interdependent life the two of you led before I came on the scene. And Kyra is worried about her own mother's feelings, which is admirable, under the circumstances, since Sheila appears to be hurting. But Kyra would never send anybody a mean-spirited cartoon."

"You have no idea what Kyra would do," Sarah said.

"I know my daughter," Ted said tersely. "Kyra's not the type to play practical jokes on people."

"You consider this a joke?"

"Of course it's a joke," Ted said. "High-school kids are always playing pranks on each other. You're far too thin-skinned, Sarah. There are plenty of interpretations you could have put on this, and you picked the worst possible one."

"What other interpretations could there be?" Sarah demanded.

"Hang loose?" her mother suggested.

"What?"

"A play on words. Hang loose. Be cool. That kind of thing. Or—I know!" She laughed, and Sarah could have sworn there was a note of relief in the laughter. Her mother had been more worried than she had let on. "The subject you chose for your history-class paper was the Salem witch-hunt. You told us yourself that you and Charlie Gorman pounced on that subject and that Charlie stripped the library of reference books. This drawing is a not very subtle message from some very irritated class-mate who also wanted the chance to write a paper on that subject."

"T-That's ridiculous," Sarah sputtered.

"Actually it wasn't a very nice thing for Charlie to do," Rosemary continued. "To take out all those books so that other students wouldn't have an opportunity to use them."

" 'All those books' means three," Sarah said. "The high-school library in this dinky little town is the pits."

"That's why it's important to get materials read and returned as quickly as possible," Ted said. "The librarian told me there was a tremendous demand for those books from students who wanted to write on the subject the teacher highlighted."

"It wasn't highlighted," Sarah said.

"Don't talk back to me," Ted said. "How are you coming with the research? Are you finished with the books yet?"

"This sketch is not by somebody who's mad about the history assignment!" Sarah exclaimed, furious at herself for having allowed the subject to be redirected. "The person who drew this sketch was not being cute! This person is vicious!"

"Oh, come on, Sarah," Ted said in exasperation. "You can't be implying that this is a death threat. Do you really think some student at Pine Crest is out to kill you?"

Sarah found herself experiencing an unexplainable pressure at her throat, as if the neck of her sweatshirt had suddenly tightened.

"Not exactly that," she said shakily. "I mean, no, of course not. Normal people don't kill each other just because they don't like each other."

"Well, I'm glad you don't believe that, because if you did it would be a sign of true paranoia," Ted said. "Rosemary, this brings me to something I've been meaning to suggest for some days now; I just haven't known how to raise the subject without upsetting you. I realize it hasn't

126

been easy for Sarah to switch high schools at the start of her senior year. I think the adjustment might be easier if she had a few sessions with the school counselor."

"I suppose that's something we ought to consider," Rosemary said slowly. She turned to Sarah. "Don't look so horrified, honey. The counseling sessions I had after your father died were all that kept me sane during that terrible time. Sometimes it takes a little professional steering to help us put things into perspective."

"I don't need—" Sarah started to respond angrily, and then forced herself to calm down and consider the suggestion. Much as she hated the thought of accepting any proposal that came from Ted, the truth was that the idea of talking to a counselor was not such a bad one. She couldn't deny that her life in Pine Crest was miserable. She knew her attitude was terrible. She had no friends, and she now realized that the boy she had halfway fallen in love with had only been using her. And the situation with her mother and Ted was so upsetting to her that she couldn't even bear to think about it. Rosemary, who was her best friend as well as her mother, had become Ted's puppet. Sarah had never felt so alone in her life. Perhaps an understanding counselor with a sympathetic ear and some wisdom to share might make her problems more tolerable.

"I guess, maybe," she said uncertainly.

"Terrific!" Ted exclaimed, obviously both surprised and pleased by this response. "I can set it up for you tomorrow. I know you'll like Mr. Lamb. Everybody does. The kids all say he's very good at helping them with their problems."

"You don't mean Misty Lamb's father!" Sarah exclaimed incredulously.

"That's right," Ted said. "I'm glad to find out you know Misty. She's the kind of girl who would make a very nice friend for you."

"Misty may be sweet, but her father's a monster," Sarah said. "You may not know it, but Misty's mother is in the hospital with a concussion because Mr. Lamb knocked her across the room."

"That's absurd!" Ted said. "The Lambs are a devoted family. Bert Lamb's wife accompanies him to faculty social functions, and I've never seen a more affectionate couple. Yes, the poor woman's in the hospital. She fell in the kitchen. But Bert had nothing to do with it. He wasn't even there. Kitchens can be hazardous places, right, Rosie?"

"So I've discovered," Rosemary said, glancing down ruefully at her bandaged arm.

"You've both of you got your heads in the sand!" Sarah told them. "This isn't the sweet little town you want to pretend it is! Terrible things are going on here! Rosemary, do you know about the bookstore that was burned down by religious fanatics?"

"I've never heard of any arson in Pine Crest," Ted said, stepping in quickly before Rosemary could answer. "There once was a bookstore that caught fire, but from everything I've heard, that was caused by a problem with the electrical system."

"I've been told that somebody deliberately set that fire," Sarah said. "The owner was sent a picture of a burning cross. That picture was a threat, not just a joke, and this picture of a gallows may be one also!"

"Forgive me, Rosemary, but I have to say this," Ted said. "Your daughter needs professional help. Listen to her ranting like a crazy person about a fine town filled with salt-of-the-earth people whom she hasn't made the slightest effort to get to know!"

"Don't you dare call me crazy!" Sarah exploded. "I know exactly what I'm saying!"

"Sarah, please, don't talk that way to Ted," Rosemary begged her. "This is his hometown and he loves it! You're hurting him deeply!"

"Aren't you taking this in?" Sarah whirled upon her mother, blinking back tears of frustration. "Rosemary, don't you get it? This is a picture of a *gallows,* a gallows that *hangs* people! Somebody drew this ghastly thing and stuck it in my locker!"

"I wouldn't be surprised if you drew it yourself," Ted said with ice in his voice. "You've been trying to sabotage my relationship with your mother from the moment we met. This is obviously a bizarre attempt to upset her so much that she'll call things off with me and take you back to California. Well, I have news for you, Sarah, your plan is not going to work. Your mother and I are in love, and whether you like it or not, we're going to make a life together. If our situation were different, I'd suggest that all three of us get family counseling from Reverend Morris, but given the circumstances that's out of the question. So Bert Lamb seems the only viable option."

"There is no way in the world that I will ever get counseling from Misty Lamb's father!" Sarah shouted, shaking with fury. "Just the thought of being alone with that man makes me nauseated! I'm going to get some fresh air before I throw up!"

She grabbed her jacket and let herself out into the night. The little town of Pine Crest lay spread out all about her, dozing in the light of a huge white moon, as deceptively peaceful and friendly-looking as a Norman

129

Rockwell painting. It struck her for the first time that it resembled old Salem Village. Of course, that village had been in New England, and this was in the Ozarks. But the size of the town and its isolation from the more progressive outside world were similar, as was the dogmatic narrow-mindedness of the residents. When she thought about what Charlie had told her about the bookstore being burned down simply because it contained books on subjects some people found objectionable, it gave her the sort of chill she had once heard described on a television talk show as "a goose walking over my grave."

She was shivering also because she was physically cold. The temperature had plummeted twenty degrees in the past week, and an early snowfall was predicted for the coming weekend. She couldn't just stand there and freeze, she needed to start moving, but she had no idea where to go. Back in California if she went for a stroll after dinner she would head straight for one of the hangouts where she and her school friends congregated. Here she didn't have that option. In Pine Crest, of course, the young people got together also. They hung out at the Burger Barn and the bowling alley; they went to movies; they gathered at one another's houses; and all of them seemed to be involved in activities at the church. The difference was that in Ventura she had been a welcome part of things, while here she was considered an intruder, although what exactly she was intruding on she hadn't figured out yet.

Arbitrarily she turned left and began to walk briskly, stomping her feet down overly hard on the sidewalk to get her blood circulating. Ahead of her loomed Garrett Hill, a dark and brooding sentinel, standing guard over the town that had been placed in its keeping. Eric had wanted to drive her up to a parking area at the top, where he had said the moonlit town would look exactly like a chessboard. In retrospect Sarah realized that the metaphor said much about Eric, who had learned, perhaps from his father, to regard the people in his life as little more than game pieces.

Although their moonlit facades did make them appear to be replicas of each other, Sarah knew the identities of the houses on either side from the paper route. This was the one with the blue shutters; the next had a holly bush by the side of the front steps; and then came the one that she often forgot to throw to because by the time they reached it she and Charlie were deep in conversation.

It occurred to her that Charlie was the only friend she had here. She looked forward to seeing him each morning and actually missed him on the weekends when his mother took over the paper-throwing. This pudgy boy whom Kyra had dismissed so derisively as the "class clown" was proving to have a depth she had not expected. Who would have thought that he listened to New Age music and sent away for books about subjects like reincarnation?

She found herself wishing that Charlie were here with her now, plodding along beside her in the worn plaid jacket with the patches on the elbows. She wondered if that was the only jacket he owned. If he had another, he never wore it. With all the talking they had done, he had never once mentioned anything about his home life, except to say that his mother needed the station wagon to get to work. She wondered how his father got to work, or if he even had a father. Perhaps, like her, he came from a single-parent family. Kyra had undoubtedly fed her that information over the walkie-talkie, but at the time she hadn't been interested enough to make note of it. The fact that it seemed so important to Charlie to hang on to his paper route suggested that the family might not be well off.

She had walked only half a block when she became aware of the sound of a car engine coming to life behind her. Her first thought was that it might be Rosemary coming after her to apologize for the scene in the living room and assure her that she believed her, no matter what Ted said.

Sarah waited for the beams of the headlights to light up the road as the car came abreast of her, but that didn't happen. The engine continued to purr softly a short distance behind her like a cat that was idly watching a bird. The driver made no attempt either to pull up beside her or to pass her. Instead he seemed to be following her.

Following her? That was ridiculous. Why would anyone do that? But of course there were creeps who mugged women who went out walking alone at night. You read about such things happening all the time in big cities, but not in small towns like Pine Crest, where everybody in town knew everybody else. But then, Pine Crest was not what it appeared on the surface. This was a town where people kept ugly secrets hidden from view behind the closed doors of their neat little homes.

There was no sense taking a chance when you didn't have to. Spinning on her heel, Sarah abruptly broke into a run, cutting across the lawn to her left and dashing through the dark space between houses like a rabbit diving into its hole. Emerging into the moonlight, she raced across the sequence of adjoining backyards, grateful that it was winter and there were no sprinklers or lawn chairs to collide with, and within minutes was in the yard behind her own house.

Standing at the door to the kitchen with her hand on the knob, she waited for her heart to stop racing and her breath to slow down before she went back inside. If she told Ted and Rosemary that she had panicked over something so innocuous, it would appear to be validation of her alleged paranoia. And with pretty good cause. Now that she thought about it, she did recall that there had been a car parked across the street from their house. It had not occurred to her to notice if there were people in it, but she couldn't say that there hadn't been. Why should she find it significant that their decision to drive off coincided with her leaving the house to take a walk? Two kids making out in the moonlight—what could be more natural? And now they were leaving, but driving away very slowly, possibly still wrapped in each other's arms. Why should she be so frightened by something so normal?

Maybe Rosemary was right, Sarah tried to tell herself. *Maybe that sketch was a joke about "hanging loose" or a nasty response from somebody who wanted our reference books.*

But in her heart Sarah knew it wasn't.

The occupants of that car had not been cuddling romantically in the moonlight. Maybe they were the ones who had left the gallows message. Maybe they had been stationed there to watch her house.

Three days later she found a dead crow in her locker.

chapter

THIRTEEN

I'm not going to scream, Sarah told herself. *I will not scream.*

She would handle this in an adult way. She would report this atrocity to somebody in authority. But who should that somebody be? Ted's classroom was right down the hall, and they were between class periods, but by now she had learned the hard way that it was useless to turn to Ted for anything.

I'll go over his head, she thought. *I'll go to the principal.*

She had never met Mr. Prue, although she had seen him at assemblies—a short, balding man with wire-rimmed glasses who wore neckties with pictures on them. All she knew about him as a person were the things that Eric had told her, which had not sounded appealing. But whatever his failings, he was, after all, the principal.

With the thought that the person who had planted the crow might be there in the crowded hall watching her, she was careful to keep her face expressionless as she went to the rest room and brought back a large wad of paper towels. By the time she had wrapped up the feathered corpse, trying her best to avoid physical contact, the third-period bell had rung and the hall had emptied out.

Carrying the bundle at arm's length, she went down the hall to the principal's office.

"I need to see Mr. Prue," she told the secretary, whose desk bore a nameplate identifying her as Mrs. Ellis.

"Do you have an appointment?" the woman asked her.

"No," Sarah said. "But it's very important that I see him."

"I'll see if he's free," Mrs. Ellis said, glancing with obvious curiosity at the package in Sarah's hands. She lifted the receiver and punched in a number. "There's a student here to see you, Mr. Prue. She seems very upset." She turned to Sarah. "Your name, dear?"

"Sarah Zoltanne."

"Sarah Zoltanne," Mrs. Ellis repeated, and then nodded at Sarah and said, "Mr. Prue says he's busy, but he can spare a couple of minutes if it's really important."

Sarah opened the door to the inner office and went in. The principal was seated behind a wide desk that was covered with piles of papers and a lineup of coffee cups bearing cute slogans such as HAVE YOU HUGGED A TEACHER TODAY? and BE SURE TO UPHOLD FINE PRINCIPALS! A photograph of a plump blond woman with a plump blond child on her lap sat to the right of the telephone. To the left of the phone, in a matching frame, there was a hand-embroidered sampler bearing the garbled quotation SUFFER THE LITTLE CHILDREN TO COME UNTO ME, FOR THEIRS IS THE KINGDOM OF HEAVEN.

There was a chair across from the desk, but Sarah didn't sit down.

"So, Sarah, you have a problem?" the principal asked pleasantly.

"I think you could say that," Sarah said. She plunked the towel-wrapped carcass down in front of him. "I found this in my locker. It's a dead bird."

"I'd appreciate it if you didn't place it on my desk," Mr. Prue said, shoving his chair back slightly and making no move to touch the package.

"It was in my locker," Sarah repeated, obligingly picking up the bundle. "Somebody got into my locker and put it there."

"Do you know who it was?" Mr. Prue asked her.

"Not specifically, no. It could have been any one of a lot of people."

"Does anybody know your locker combination?"

"Not that I know of, but I have a lower locker, so I guess somebody could have stood behind me without my realizing it and watched me while I dialed the combination."

"I can see why you're upset," Mr. Prue said. "Nobody would want to be greeted by something like that. If you knew who did it, I'd call them in and talk to them. But since you don't, there's not much I can do." He paused and then said, "You're a new student, aren't you? The one who just moved here recently from California? Your mother submitted an application to teach here."

"Yes," Sarah said.

"You were in the Halloween carnival. You had a Gypsy act, didn't you? A fortune-telling booth?"

"Yes," Sarah said again.

"I almost called you in to talk to you about that, Sarah," Mr. Prue said solemnly. "We have a very strict policy that our carnival not contain anything that involves the occult. That was one of the specifications agreed upon between the school board and the senior class when they first applied for permission to put on this annual fund-raiser. Eric Garrett explained to me that when you asked him if you could have a booth, he didn't realize what you were planning to do in it."

"What!" Sarah exclaimed, unable to believe what she was hearing. "I didn't approach Eric about it, it was *Eric* who approached *me*! He and Kyra Thompson—"

"As president of the class, Eric felt it was his duty to encourage a new student to participate in school events," Mr. Prue continued as if he had not heard her. "He thought you were going to be running an Apple on the String game. By the time he realized what you were actually doing, it was too late for him to stop you. The carnival was already in progress, and he didn't want to embarrass you in front of all your classmates.

"I considered calling you in to discuss the matter, but it was water under the bridge, so I decided to let it go. But since you've now come in to see me of your own accord, I feel I should take this opportunity to clarify our standards. I realize people are different out in California. They have a whole different mind-set out there—crime and violence, nude beaches, unusual religious sects, same-sex marriages, I don't know what all. But here in Pine Crest we are—I suppose some would call it—*conservative* in our attitudes and our practices. I call it moral. This is a Christian community with a Christian value system."

"There's nothing very Christian about this," Sarah said shakily, gesturing with the wad of towels, through which blood was now beginning to seep.

"A lot of high jinks go on among high-school students," Mr. Prue told her. "They're always playing pranks

137

on each other. Just a matter of weeks ago somebody left a fish in another student's locker. He was a good sport about it and accepted it as a joke."

"This wasn't a joke," Sarah said. "Somebody killed a bird in order to do this. They did it out of hatred, not as a joke."

"Perhaps you should ask yourself what you might have done to arouse that sort of feeling in people," Mr. Prue said. "Did you arrive here in Pine Crest with a superior attitude that offends your new classmates? Have you hurt people's feelings by making them feel inferior? Have you wronged anyone, either intentionally or unintentionally? If this isn't a joke, then it's obviously the reaction of somebody who feels he or she has a strong and legitimate grievance. Could it be related to the fortune-telling? Something that you said to someone that hurt his or her feelings?"

"I don't know," Sarah said, averting her eyes. His off-the-cuff guess had jabbed her in a spot where she was vulnerable; she could not deny that she had told fortunes that had upset people.

"Don't look away when I ask you a question," Mr. Prue said sharply. "It makes it appear as if you have something to be ashamed of."

Sarah glanced up into eyes that, magnified by the lenses of his glasses, seemed suddenly horribly familiar.

"I don't know," she repeated nervously. "I guess it's possible."

"You must also realize, there has been talk—not gossip exactly, but some speculation—about the reason your mother chose to relocate to Pine Crest," Mr. Prue continued. "Not for exactly the best of motives, shall we say? Those kinds of things have a way of catching up with people. Not that you were responsible, of course. You're an innocent victim of the fallout, as children often are. In the case of the student who was gifted with a fish in his locker, there was an issue over which his parents had aroused the ire of the community. Not that this excused retaliation against the student, but children are bound to mirror the emotions of their parents. It might not be a bad idea to discuss this unfortunate episode with your mother. Most loving parents—and I am sure your mother is loving, as all mothers are—do not want their beloved children to suffer the consequences of their own ill-advised actions.

"I've known Ted Thompson and his lovely family all my life. Ted is one of our most respected teachers, and Sheila is the pillar of our church. All marriages go through times of shakiness, particularly when the husband goes through what is often termed middle-age crisis and becomes vulnerable to outside influences. But if left alone, most couples manage to work their way through those problem times and become even closer for having done so. I think you understand what I'm getting at."

"No," Sarah said. "Exactly what are you getting at?"

"Only that if you should make your mother aware of the problems she is causing for you, she might weigh her actions more carefully. Now, go on with your normal day and keep a smile on your face. Try to act as if they haven't gotten to you, and when they don't get a reaction, this kind of teasing usually stops in a jiffy. The boy who found the fish in his locker just laughed about it. The fact that he was so good-natured stopped things right there. There hasn't been another such incident."

As Sarah turned to leave, he added, "You'd better dispose of that thing promptly. Dead birds carry all kinds of diseases."

"What should I do with it?" Sarah asked him. "Drop it in a wastebasket?"

"Certainly not. We don't want it here in the school building. Put it in the garbage bin behind the cafeteria. Oh, and on your way out, ask Mrs. Ellis to write you a tardy excuse for your next class."

Stunned by the finality of his response, Sarah did as directed, stopping at the secretary's desk to collect a tardy excuse. Then, moving like a zombie, she went out to the bin behind the lunchroom and opened the lid. The stench of rotting food rose to fill her nostrils, and bile surged into the back of her throat, threatening to strangle her. Struggling to keep from vomiting, she dropped the soggy bundle on top of a pile of moldy pasta and slammed the lid closed.

"May God have mercy on your soul," she whispered to the crow.

The thought of going to class, presenting her excuse, and turning to face her fellow students, most of whom probably knew why she was late and were eagerly anticipating her reaction, was intolerable. But so was going home to face Rosemary, who would assume that she was sick and insist on dosing her with orange juice and aspirin.

It was all too much. Leaning against the garbage bin, she buried her face in her hands and let the tears come.

"Sarah?" a voice asked softly. "Are you okay?"

"What are you doing out here?" Sarah choked out the question without uncovering her face. "You're supposed to be in history class."

"I got to school late," Charlie said. "My dad had a doctor's appointment. We only have one car, so I had to drop Mom off at work and take Dad to the doctor and

140

then take him home after. When I got to school, I saw you down at the end of the hall headed out the back door. What's going on?"

"Somebody left a dead crow in my locker," Sarah said bluntly.

"A *crow*? You mean like a bird? They put a dead *bird* in your locker?"

"It's no worse than a fish," Sarah snapped, lowering her hands and glaring at him through her tears. She felt immediately ashamed of herself when she saw his round face flush crimson. "I'm sorry, that was horrid of me. Let's face it, I'm a horrid person. Mr. Prue said this is all my fault. If I was nicer, people would like me better and this wouldn't have happened."

"You're the nicest person I know," Charlie said gently.

"You're not going to find many people agreeing with you," Sarah said. "The crow is just a part of it. A couple of days ago somebody put a picture in my locker. It was a sketch of a gallows. Yes, a *gallows,*" she repeated when she saw his startled expression, "like they used to hang witches. And now they're giving me the same sick message with the crow. Birds, like cats, were supposed to have been witches' familiars—evil, satanic creatures in league with the devil. I can't believe I chose that topic to write about! It's reached a point where it makes me feel queasy just to think about it."

"I know what you mean," Charlie said. "I can't deal with it either. It was bad enough reading that over two hundred people were imprisoned, but when I got to the part about Giles Corey being pressed to death with stones, I suddenly found I couldn't breathe. I mean that literally—I thought I was going to pass out. I realize now that

I never should have chosen that topic. The only reason I was drawn to it was because it was highlighted."

"It wasn't highlighted," Sarah said.

"It was printed in boldface."

"No, it wasn't. I saw it that way too at first, but I was mistaken."

"That's not what the librarian says," Charlie said. "She stopped me the other day when I was passing in the hall and asked me to get those books back as soon as possible, because almost everybody wants to write papers on the witch trials. They said that topic was printed in boldface on the handout sheet."

"Ted said that too," Sarah said. "I don't understand it. It's just another weird thing on top of all of the rest of them. I hate this school, and I hate this mean little town! I know it's unfair, but I can't forgive Rosemary for bringing me here."

"Did you ever wonder why she did that?" Charlie asked her.

"It's because she fell head-over-heels crazy in love with Ted Thompson."

"And why did she do that? What's so irresistible about Mr. Thompson?"

"Nothing that I can see. He's a tyrant."

"Does your mother have a history of doing this sort of thing? Going off the deep end over married tyrants?"

"Absolutely not! This was totally out of character. My mother has always been independent and self-confident. When she's gone out with men, it's been on her own terms; she's never let anybody dominate her. I don't get it."

"Which makes you wonder what's really behind this," Charlie said. "Maybe, in her subconscious, she knew that she was meant to bring you to Pine Crest, because you had karma to fulfill here."

"Karma?" Sarah said. "That's one of those reincarnation terms."

"Do you know much about reincarnation?" Charlie asked her.

"Just that the theory is that people live more than once."

"There's more to it than that," Charlie said. "The concept is that this earth is a kind of schoolhouse, and our lesson plans are laid out for us before birth. We know what they are, but that knowledge is buried in our subconscious. Sometimes it emerges during therapy. Psychologists sometimes use hypnosis to bring it to the surface so their patients will understand their compulsions. Now, hear me out, don't close your mind to this too quickly. Maybe, subconsciously, your mother knew it was part of her prebirth game plan to bring you to Pine Crest because you have karma here that you have to deal with. Mr. Thompson just punched the buttons to put her into action."

"Are you trying to tell me I'm here to be punished?" Sarah asked in horror.

"Not at all," Charlie said. "Karma isn't a punishment, it's a teaching aid. The idea behind reincarnation is that for most of us one lifetime isn't enough to learn all the spiritual lessons we're signed up for. Karma gives us a chance to retake the classes we flunk. If we mess things up in one lifetime, we're allowed to come back and experience a similar situation—maybe from another angle—so we can learn the lessons we didn't get the first time."

"That's an interesting idea," Sarah said, "but it's pretty far out."

"It's the basis of all Eastern religions, and most early

Christians believed it. The Gnostic scriptures quote Jesus as saying, 'Souls are poured from one into another of different bodies of the world.' "

"What does that have to do with the crow?"

"Maybe something, maybe nothing," Charlie said. "What did Mr. Prue suggest that you do about it?"

"Consider it a practical joke."

"Mr. Prue is a jerk. I say go to your folks."

"I don't have folks, remember? I just have my mother."

"Like it or not, you also have Mr. Thompson. He's a teacher, he's got to be aware of the stuff that goes on here. He might shrug off the sketch, but he wouldn't expect you to put up with a bloody crow in your locker. That's not only sick, the person who did that could be dangerous."

"Ted would want to know why the cheerleaders hate me," Sarah said. "I can't explain that without telling him about the fortune-telling. He'll be furious, and Rosemary too, especially when they find out I stole Ted's key and was holding the sessions in his apartment."

"You'll just have to tell them and take the fallout," Charlie said. "It's not like you have much choice. But as far as our reports go, this is definitely not the subject for you and me to be writing about. We've got to switch topics."

"We can't," Sarah said. "It's too late to start researching something else."

"I wrote a paper on the Boston Tea Party for a tenth-grade social studies class," Charlie said. "I think I still have the first draft in one of my old notebooks. I'll polish it up and use it again for this class—Mrs. Larkin won't know it's a rerun—and you can write your own paper from my notes. We won't get As, but at least we won't get Fs."

He threw a friendly arm around her shoulders and gently

but firmly drew her away from the garbage bin. "Let's go get a milk shake."

"You mean cut school?"

"Were you planning to go to class?"

"Well, no—but you—"

"It'll be good for my physique," Charlie said. "The milk shakes at the Burger Barn are made with yogurt. If I drink enough of them, I might get skinny."

The statement was so absurd that Sarah couldn't help smiling.

"Do you know, I've never been to the Burger Barn?" she said. "It's where everybody here goes on dates, and except for one movie with Eric, which I realize now was a sop to keep me pacified, I haven't had one single date since I got here."

"Neither have I," Charlie said. "So this will be a first for us. What a boost for my ego—a date with the fabulous Madam Zoltanne! And I've even got Mom's car, so I can drive you in style to the take-out window!"

His arm around her shoulders was sturdy and comforting, and he didn't remove it as he walked her out to the student parking lot.

FOURTEEN

"I've never heard such a load of nonsense in my life," Ted said.

Sarah stared at him in astonishment. As before, she had waited until after dinner to shatter her mother's evening, but as soon as the last of the plates had been loaded into the dishwasher, she poured out the whole sordid story. Not only did she describe the incident with the crow, but she also told them about everything that had led up to it, including Eric's proposal that they start a fortune-telling business and Kyra's participation by supplying information.

"She gave me things to tell people that she knew would make them furious," she said. "That's why they've branded me a witch. They probably chose the crow to leave in my locker because witches are supposed to use birds for familiars."

She was braced for her mother's hurt and disillusionment and expected Ted to be furious, and justifiably so. After all, she and Eric had physically invaded his apartment and thereby made him a part of a scam that would be abhorrent to him. The one thing she was not prepared for was his refusal to believe her.

"Why would I lie about something like that?" she demanded.

"For the same reason you showed us that sketch of a gallows," Ted said. "To get your mother to move back to your beloved Ventura. Ever since you got here, you've been whining about how miserable you are. To hear you talk, you'd think you'd been thrown into a snake pit. You've been feeding Rosemary one pitiful story after another: Just being in this town gives you nightmares and makes you scream in your sleep; the kids are unfriendly; people put mean pictures in your locker. Now you're asking us to believe that your classmates are out to get you by putting dead creatures in your locker because you've been conducting a fortune-telling scam out of *my* apartment and that both my daughter and the president of the class have been involved in it. You've gone over the line, Sarah. Your mother and I weren't born yesterday."

"Don't condemn her so fast, Ted," Rosemary said. "These are serious accusations. If what Sarah says is true, this is a nasty situation."

"A few well-placed phone calls will make this or break this," Ted said. "We'll start with Eric Garrett."

He looked up the number in the book, then picked up the phone and dialed.

"Hello, John? Ted Thompson here. How are things going? . . . Glad to hear it. . . . Nope, no legal problems, thank goodness. If there were, I'd be phoning you at your office. I wondered if Eric was around. If so, I'd like to speak to him. . . . I see. Well, if it's not too late when he gets in, would you have him give me a call? I'm at Rosemary Zoltanne's house. I think Eric knows the number.

Oh, and while I'm at it, I want you to know how grateful I am to your son for his emergency treatment of Rosemary when she burned herself a couple of weeks ago. You ought to be grooming that boy of yours for medical school. . . . Just kidding, John, just kidding! He's going to make a terrific attorney, just like his dad. Have him call me, okay? There's something I need to ask him. . . . Thanks, John. Give my best to Nancy. Goodbye."

He replaced the receiver on the hook and immediately lifted it again. The next number he dialed from memory.

"Hello, Sheila? It's Ted. . . . I agree, that was unnecessary. Of course you know my voice. I'd like to speak to Kyra. . . . No, it's not about Thanksgiving. However, since I've got you on the line, is there any chance that Kyra and Brian—? . . . Well, look, we'll talk about it later. Right now I need to talk to Kyra about something else. . . . No, I won't go into it with you. It's between my daughter and me. May I please speak to her?" He waited in obvious irritation until Kyra got on the phone. The conversation that followed was a short one. "Kyra, what do you know about a fortune-telling scam that Sarah and Eric Garrett were conducting out of my apartment? Sarah says you were providing her with information so that she could fake the fortunes. . . . No, of course, I didn't believe her, but Sarah's been very insistent, and in the interest of fairness I felt I had to ask you. . . . I realize that. It made no sense to me either. I'll talk to you tomorrow. We need to discuss Thanksgiving, but tonight isn't a good time for that. . . . Okay, baby. I'm sorry if I upset you. Sleep tight."

He hung up the phone and turned to face Sarah and Rosemary.

"Kyra says she knows nothing about it."

148

"She's lying!" Sarah exclaimed.

"She says that you and she are so hostile toward each other that the last thing she would ever want to do would be to get involved in any sort of business venture with you. Rosie, be honest, now, can you picture our daughters teaming up like that?"

"It *is* hard to imagine," Rosemary admitted.

"Right you are. But for the sake of argument, let's say that Kyra is the one who's lying. Maybe she did supply all this inflammatory information. But what would her reason be? She doesn't need spending money. I give her a good allowance, as I would Sarah if she weren't too hard-nosed to accept it. Eric certainly doesn't need money—he has everything he needs and more. His father even bought him a car for his sixteenth birthday and pays for the gas. Beyond that, how could Sarah have provided information about things that hadn't happened yet? Grace Rice's elopement with her sister's boyfriend? Misty Lamb's mother falling in the kitchen? Did Kyra tell you all that too, Sarah?"

"No," Sarah said, her heart sinking.

"Then where did it come from?"

Sarah shot her mother a look of desperation.

"It seemed like I was seeing those things in the ball."

"In the crystal paperweight?"

"Yes, I saw them in the paperweight."

"Is that the same paperweight your mother let you use at the carnival?"

"There's only one paperweight. I have it on my desk."

"Did it show you the future when you were telling fortunes at the school?"

"No," Sarah said. "I mean—well, there was one thing: I thought I saw somebody trip Charlie, but that turned out

149

not to be true. The fact that he fell that night was apparently a coincidence."

"Okay, let's go back a few paces. You say you were conducting this scam out of my apartment. So, show me the duplicate key you used to get in there."

"I gave it to Eric," Sarah said.

"That's convenient, now, isn't it?"

"But, Ted, what about the crow?" Rosemary asked, breaking into the conversation. "We can chalk up the drawing as a prank, but not a dead bird. Somebody actually slaughtered a living creature and then went to the effort of finding out Sarah's locker combination and putting the dreadful thing in there for her to find. And Sarah's right, birds do symbolize witchcraft. They're considered 'familiars,' animal friends who assist witches in their work. The symbol of a dead bird could be a symbol of a dead witch. And if uneducated, superstitious hoodlums have labeled Sarah a *witch*—"

"The children in this town where I was born and raised and have taught school for all of my adult life are not 'uneducated hoodlums,'" Ted said angrily. "They are a lot less superstitious than the flower-child types in California who chant meaningless gibberish and practice yoga and burn incense. And who is to say that Sarah *did* find a bird in her locker? It's hard for you to accept, I'm sure, but your daughter needs help, Rosie. I'm going to insist that she get counseling."

"I won't go to Mr. Lamb!" Sarah said adamantly. "That man needs counseling himself! He's a wife abuser!"

"May I ask how you came up with that slanderous tidbit? And please, don't tell me again that you saw it in a paperweight."

"I got it from Kyra," Sarah said. "Then Misty confirmed it. The reason she came to have her fortune told was because she was afraid for her mother's life. She wanted to know if she would ever have the courage to leave her father."

"The Lambs are a happily married couple," Ted said. "At last year's faculty Christmas party they were holding hands like newlyweds. And even if I didn't trust my daughter's word, which I do with all my heart, there is no way that she would have access to personal information of that nature."

"She got it from her mother," Sarah said. "It was in the church files."

"You want me to believe that *Sheila* is a part of this alleged con scheme? It will be a cold day in hell before I buy *that*, Sarah. My wife may have her problems, but one thing I will say for her is that she is a highly moral woman. There is no way in this world that Sheila Thompson would become involved in anything that had to do with the occult."

"Call Mr. Prue," Sarah said, giving up on the subject of Kyra. "He'll tell you I came into his office today with the crow."

"I plan to do exactly that," Ted said, and picked up the receiver again.

This phone call was even briefer than the last one, and after the initial question Ted listened in silence. When he hung up the phone, he was shaking his head.

"Mr. Prue says, yes, Sarah did come to his office this morning," he said, addressing himself to Rosemary as if Sarah wasn't there. "He says she was hostile and hysterical, and he, too, feels she would benefit from counseling. He never actually saw any crow. She was carrying a bundle of papers in which she said there was the carcass of a bird, but she wouldn't open it. He thinks that it's very doubtful there was anything in it."

"I tried to show him!" Sarah cried. "He didn't want to look at it! He wanted it off his desk because he was afraid of germs!"

The telephone rang. Sarah grabbed for the receiver before Ted could reach for it. As she had anticipated, it was Eric returning Ted's call.

"It's about the fortune-telling, Eric," she said hurriedly before Ted could intercept the phone call. "I've told Ted and Rosemary everything. Now I need for you to verify it."

There was a long pause, and then Eric said softly, "I trusted you."

Sarah felt herself starting to falter at the hurt in his voice. Was it possible that she was mistaken and Eric really *did* care? But if so, how could he have lied about her to Mr. Prue? Or had Mr. Prue been the liar and misquoted Eric as saying she was the one who'd initiated the fortune-telling?

"I'm not out to get you into trouble," she said. "I mean that, Eric. I'm willing to accept the blame for getting us into Ted's apartment. Other than trespassing, we weren't doing anything illegal, so, please, just tell him the truth and make him believe me."

She handed the receiver to Ted.

"So—what about it?" Ted asked in the classroom voice she had come to despise. "Were you and Sarah and Kyra running a fortune-telling scam? . . . You heard me right, I said a *fortune-telling* scam. Telling people's fortunes for money. . . . No, I don't mean the game at the carnival. I mean a private moneymaking business run out of my apartment. . . . Then why would Sarah say so? It makes no sense. Why confess to something that none of you were doing?"

He listened for a moment.

"I see," he said finally with a note of relief in his voice. Then, to Sarah's astonishment, he chuckled. "Well, that explains it. It's tough being a teenage heartthrob, but somebody has to do it. Thanks for returning my call, I really appreciate it. I'll see you in class. Don't forget the quiz on Monday—not that a student of your caliber needs any reminding."

He hung up the phone and sat for a moment in silence.

Then he said, "He denied knowing anything about a fortune-telling business. Sarah, I think you'd better give up on this story. All you're going to do is dig yourself in deeper and deeper."

"What did he say when you asked him my motive for lying?" Sarah asked hopelessly, too heartsick to argue any further.

"He explained that you're angry because he told you he couldn't date you any longer because he and Kyra are going to be going steady. He said you threatened to retaliate, but he never imagined you'd go this far. This is very disturbing, Sarah. I find it incredible that you would throw yourself on the funeral pyre, so to speak, in order to get revenge on Eric and Kyra. I've heard the old adage 'Hell hath no fury like a woman scorned,' but I never expected to see it played out in my own home."

"Ted, that's cruel and unnecessary," Rosemary objected. "If what Eric says is true, then Sarah has a right to be hurt. He's been leading her on, taking her out at least once or twice a week, and calling her on the phone almost every evening."

"He's a kind young man," Ted said. "I wish there were

153

more like him. He could see that Sarah was having trouble making friends here and wanted to make her feel welcome. You're talking as if Kyra jumped in out of the blue and broke up a big romance. Kyra and Eric have been bosom buddies all their lives. Eric's mother was and still is Sheila's best friend."

"So now we're back to Sheila again," Rosemary said. "Is it possible that this whole thing is a ploy of hers to come between you and me by way of our children?"

"Don't try to blame Sheila for your daughter's bizarre behavior," Ted shot back at her. "The next thing you're going to be saying is that Sheila sneaked into the school building and planted a bird in Sarah's locker, an invisible bird that nobody but Sarah has seen."

"I'm not saying that at all," Rosemary said, her voice quivering. "I'm just saying that it's not as easy to make friends in this town as you pretend it is. The people here have all known each other forever, and Sarah has been so lonely—"

"Please, Rosemary, let it drop," Sarah said. "My loneliness isn't the issue. The issue is that somebody left me a dead crow. That's the bottom line. If you and Ted need proof, then go over to the school and dig through the garbage bin. You'll find the disgusting thing about a third of the way down. You'd better wear rubber gloves, because by now it's probably got maggots."

"Now I suppose you're going to stalk out of the room," Ted said. "That's what you always do when you don't like the way the conversation is going."

Sarah didn't bother to answer. She was afraid that if she tried to respond, she would cry.

She got her jacket off the coat tree in the hall and opened the front door. It was there again—a car parked directly across the street. Was this the same car that had followed her from the house? That question could not be answered, as she had fled without turning to look at it. She strained her eyes in an effort to see it more clearly, but clouds covered the sky, blotting out the moon like shutters, and all she could make out was the car's dark shape against the curb. She couldn't even tell how many people were in it, or if indeed there was anybody in it at all. But if not, why would it be parked there? The people who lived in that house always parked in their driveway.

They've staked out our home, Sarah thought with a jolt of terror. *It wasn't just a one-time thing, they're doing it every night!*

She was tempted to run back to the living room and drag her mother and Ted to the door. "Come, look! This is evidence!" she would tell them. But evidence of *what?* There was nothing overtly threatening about a car parked on a public street. She could already hear Ted's reaction: "How paranoid can you get, Sarah? Do you think they're carrying Uzis?"

Was the car empty or was it occupied? It was impossible to tell. As her eyes became better adjusted to the darkness, she thought she saw movement on the driver's side, but she couldn't be sure. She contemplated crossing the street to establish that for certain, but didn't have the courage. That was probably just what they hoped for. They knew that she was aware that they were out there, because here she stood, framed in a brightly lit doorway, staring straight across at them. Were they waiting there for her curiosity to get the best of her and bring her out into the night to offer herself up to them? Or was it strictly her imagination that the interior of the car now suddenly seemed churning with activity, as if it were filled with people, shifting position on the seats to get a better look at her?

A small black missile came streaking out of the darkness as if propelled by a demon's slingshot. Sarah opened her mouth to scream, and then, as the creature wrapped itself around her ankles, she began to giggle in hysterical relief.

"What are you running from?" she asked. "Do they scare you too?"

She bent and gathered up Yowler, clutching him tightly against her chest, gathering comfort from his furry warmth.

"My security dolly," she whispered. "I should have named you Dorcas." She buried her face in his neck and giggled even harder. She was losing control, and felt as if she might be going crazy. Or maybe she already was crazy. Did crazy people realize they had lost their senses? Was it possible she was insane and just didn't know it? Could something have snapped in her brain one night while she was sleeping so that she woke up in the morning no longer able to discriminate between what was real and what was imaginary?

"Sarah!" Ted called from the living room. "Either go out or stay in, but shut that door. You're letting in the cold."

Sarah closed the door and carefully locked it. Then, with Yowler still in her arms, she went down the hall to her bedroom. The essence of Kyra came billowing out to greet her, even though Kyra's physical self was elsewhere. The scent of her cloying perfume had seeped into the curtains and bedspreads so that, with every breath that Sarah took, Kyra seemed to be invading her lungs. Kyra's rosebud pajamas lay tossed in a heap on her pillow, despite the fact that there was a perfectly good drawer for her to put them in, and the top of the bureau was littered with her half-used lipsticks and little jars of freckle cream. A splotch of her tacky pink nail polish decorated the throw rug between the beds, like blood from an anemic vampire.

Very deliberately Sarah placed Yowler on Kyra's bed.

"Shed on the pillow!" she directed him.

Yowler immediately leaped down, as if he wanted no contact with the bed, and Sarah didn't blame him.

Thinking of the car across the street, she adjusted the window blinds so that there was no possible way anyone could see in. Then she placed a tape in her player and adjusted the volume, filling the room with the dreamy lilt of panpipes and the soothing ripple of a harp. She switched off the overhead fixture and clicked on the bedside lamp, draping Kyra's pajamas over the shade to dim the light.

Then she went over to her desk and picked up the paperweight.

"Here goes nothing," she told herself nervously as she deliberately stared into its depths, willing the pictures to come even as she dreaded them.

"Show me the faces of the people in that car," she said softly, to whom she did not know. To the ball itself? To God? To her own subconscious? "Show me their faces," she whispered again. "I want to see their faces."

It might have been minutes, it might have been hours, before it happened. All she knew was that her head was beginning to ache and her eyes were blurring with the strain of keeping them focused on the center of nothing, when the strange gray swirls began to appear in the glass. She held her breath as she watched them shifting about— forming, dissolving, and re-forming like clouds in a windstorm—until at last a picture began to appear to her, a picture that she had not asked for.

With a moan of horror she let the ball drop from her hands.

The picture was of a girl with long dark hair—a tall, slender girl who looked very much like Sarah.

The girl had a noose around her neck.

chapter
FIFTEEN

She tried not to fall asleep, because she did not want to dream, and she could tell by the tug of her eyelids that a dream awaited her. It was there ahead of her, poised at the edge of her mind, impatient for the bars of consciousness to drop so that it could attack her.

Her eyelids won, and she finally let them fall closed. The instant her brain let go, the dream was upon her, angry at having been kept waiting, sucking her into its depths and making her a part of it.

She was standing at the edge of a crowd, but—wait—was she *standing*? No, she was seated on shoulders—the broad, strong shoulders of somebody who loved her, for the hands that were gripping her ankles were gentle and reassuring.

In front of her, teetering on the topmost rung of a ladder, there stood a woman with a hangman's noose around her neck. The other end of the rope was looped around the branch of a massive oak tree. From her seat on high, Sarah could look across the heads of the people in front of her and stare straight into the woman's terrified eyes.

This was not the girl in the crystal ball; this woman was older and frailer, with pallid skin, as if deprived of the sun for months. Still, when the woman glared back at her, Sarah knew her, and the hatred she saw in those eyes transcended the fear in them.

"I want to get down!" Sarah whimpered. "Papa, please, put me down!"

But the man on whose shoulders she sat did not seem to hear her.

"This is a day of celebration!" he was shouting. "Blessings upon you, my brethren! Our Lord awarded you the duty of exposing and destroying those worshipers of Satan, who have dwelt among us disguised as our friends and neighbors, and you have obeyed His commandment!"

"I didn't mean it," Sarah whispered. "I didn't really mean it."

But again the man did not hear her.

He turned to the woman on the ladder and bellowed, *"Confess, witch!"*

"I am no more a witch than you are, Reverend!" the woman screamed at him.

There followed a moment of silence in which it seemed that nobody breathed, a moment in which all motion appeared to be suspended, as if a projector had frozen on a single frame of a movie too horrible to continue. Then the projector abruptly sprang back into action as the hangman shoved the woman from the ladder and the hysterical cheers of the crowd blasted Sarah awake.

Those sounds continued as she lay there, shuddering in the darkness, wondering if she had brought back the sound track from the dream and would continue to hear it ringing in her ears for all eternity. Then, with relief, she realized that she was hearing Yowler, who was making the distinctive demands for attention that had earned him his name.

Still shaken and sick from the nightmare, Sarah got out of bed and stumbled across the dark bedroom to the door and down the hall to let the cat out into the front yard. Then she returned to bed, and again felt sleep overwhelming her, but this time she gratefully sank into dreamless oblivion. She slept the rest of the night as heavily as if she had been drugged with sleeping pills, waking again at last to a rap on her door.

When she didn't respond, the door opened and Rosemary came in.

"Sarah," she asked softly, "are you all right?"

"I'm fine," Sarah said in a voice muffled with sleep.

"You normally don't sleep in like this. It's after eleven."

"I didn't sleep well last night," Sarah said. "I'm catching up."

"Ted and I are getting ready to take his kids out to lunch. Are you sure you don't want to come with us?"

"After last night?" Sarah asked incredulously.

"I just thought—oh, honey, I'm sorry that things got out of hand that way. There has to be some explanation. . . ."

"There is," Sarah said. "It's that everybody else is lying, and I'm telling the truth. The truth right now is that I want to go back to sleep." She flipped over onto her side with her back to her mother, and after a long period of silence she heard the door click closed.

She tried to burrow back into sleep, but this time it was impossible. She finally gave up the effort and simply lay there with her eyes closed, listening for sounds of Ted and

Rosemary's departure. It was only after she heard Ted's car go crunching out of the driveway that she got up and opened the blinds. The broad light of day revealed nothing fearsome, either outside or inside the bedroom. There was no mysterious vehicle stationed at the curb. The nightmare had been only a replay of a chapter from a book that she planned never to open again. The paperweight lay on the desk where she had dropped it the night before, an innocent globe of clear crystal, converting the sunbeams that streamed through the window into rainbows.

Sarah pulled on jeans and a sweatshirt and went out to the kitchen. A box of doughnuts sat open on the table, and Rosemary had left a pot of coffee on the warmer. Yowler appeared out of nowhere, demanding his own brunch. She poured herself a cup of coffee and sipped it as she opened a can of cat food.

Everything seemed so normal. The tick of the wall clock that had been in their kitchen in California. The aroma of Rosemary's overly strong coffee, enhanced with a dash of vanilla. The purr of the tattered-eared cat, reacting to the buzz of the electric can opener. Was it possible that last night had been as terrifying as she remembered?

"It was all in my head," Sarah told herself, knowing that it wasn't.

A friendly *ding-dong* shattered the silence of the house.

Sarah jumped at the unexpected sound. In the three months they had lived there, the only time she had heard the sound of the doorbell was when Eric had come by to pick her up. Aside from that, there had been nobody who called on them, not even a cosmetics salesman or a door-to-door missionary. For all practical purposes, she and her mother were pariahs.

Setting the coffee cup down, she went into the entrance

162

hall and peered out through the peephole. The face she saw there, distorted as if seen through the wrong end of a telescope, was nevertheless familiar and nonthreatening.

She quickly unlocked the door and opened it.

"Whatever you're selling, we don't want any," she said to Charlie, trying not to reveal how glad she was to see him.

"Oh, I think you do," he said easily. "I got my paycheck this morning, and I'm here to fill your wallet with beautiful green stuff. Besides, I couldn't wait until Monday to hear what happened when you told your folks about the crow."

"Come on in," Sarah said. "I've got the house to myself for a change." She led him back to the kitchen and motioned him into a chair. "Help yourself to a doughnut. I'm really glad you came by. But—number one, you don't have to fill my wallet; let's split the money. And—number two—Ted didn't believe a thing I told him. Not about the crow, and not even about the fortune-telling. As for my mother, she didn't stick up for me. I couldn't prove anything. Eric and Kyra denied everything."

"I'll back you up," Charlie said.

"That wouldn't do any good. You didn't see the crow, I just told you about it, and you never went to Ted's apartment. For all you know, I was making everything up. The worst of it is, I think Ted's convinced my mother that I'm crazy. No, actually, that's *not* the worst of it." She forced herself to speak the words that had been lurking like monsters in a hidden closet of her mind. "The worst of it is that I'm starting to believe that he's right."

"That's stupid," Charlie said. "You're anything but crazy."

"If I'm not, then that's even worse." Sarah's voice was

163

shaking. "That would mean I'm a witch, just like Debbie and Misty and the rest of them seem to think I am. When I stare into that crystal ball, I *see* things! It's not a pretense, Charlie! I mean, some of it is, but not all of it. I see future events, and they *happen!*"

"I know," Charlie said.

"You *know*? But how——?"

"When you told my fortune at the carnival, you looked into that ball and saw somebody trip me. It startled you so much that you couldn't even finish the reading."

"But I was wrong," Sarah said. "You told me you stumbled on the stairs."

"I lied," Charlie said.

"You lied!" Sarah exclaimed. "But why? Were you trying to protect somebody?"

"Myself." Charlie couldn't meet her eyes. "Even fat people have their pride. It's embarrassing to admit to a pretty girl that you're the school goat that the kids play tricks on."

"Then I *am* a witch," Sarah whispered, beginning to tremble. No wonder her classmates were drawing back from her in horror! No wonder they wanted to drive her out of their town!

"That's ridiculous," Charlie said, "You're no more a witch than those people who were hanged in Salem. The people who convicted them were victims of mass hysteria. When they came to their senses, they realized the 'afflicted children' were liars. In the next set of trials everybody was found innocent, and Governor Phips released all the people who were in prison."

"But if this thing that I'm doing isn't witchcraft, then what is it?"

"It's called scrying," Charlie said. "Like I told you once,

164

the crystal ball has no magical powers. It's just a tool for meditation."

"I don't understand," Sarah said, feeling slightly less terrified. "What's 'scrying'? I've never even heard of it."

"Lots of people see visions when they stare into shiny surfaces like crystals, or mirrors, or bodies of water," Charlie explained. "Remember how the West Indian servant taught Betty Parris and her cousin how to break an egg into a glass of water to see visions of their future husbands? They were using the white of an egg in a clear container as a substitute for a crystal ball. When people stare into something intently like that, they're more than likely to see images. For people with psychic ability, those images may sometimes reflect past or future events. There's nothing supernatural about it, it's just what happens."

"Do you think I have psychic ability?"

"I guess you must," Charlie said matter-of-factly. "It runs in families. Do your parents or grandparents have it?"

"Not that I know of, but it's not impossible," Sarah said. "The paperweight belonged to a grandmother who died before I was born, so I have no idea what she used it for. You said *past* or future events?"

"It could go either way, I guess, though it's usually precognitive."

"But a person *might* see a vision of something that's already happened?"

"That's certainly possible."

Sarah drew a long breath of relief. If the image of the girl in the noose was a vision from the past, then the resemblance to her might only have been coincidence.

"How do you know about things like that?" she asked Charlie.

"I read," he told her. "My folks have a lot of books. I told you about that catalog I get from Arizona. I sent away for a home study course on tape, and that got me on their mailing list."

"What kind of home study course?" Sarah asked with interest.

"Weight loss by self-hypnosis," Charlie said with embarrassment. "Needless to say, the tapes didn't do the job. I got pretty good at hypnosis—even got my mom to stop smoking—but I couldn't make it work for myself. I figure I must have brought these extra pounds into the world from a former lifetime, and I won't be able to get rid of them until I complete my karma. I sure hope I get that done before I'm too old to enjoy all the perks of being handsome. I liked that reading you did about my jaunt on the cruise ship."

"You're joking," Sarah said.

"For a change I'm serious."

"I can't believe you actually believe in reincarnation!"

"There's been a lot of research on the subject that's pretty convincing," Charlie said. "Would you like to trade in that witch-hunt book for a reincarnation book?"

"I have to admit you've made me curious," Sarah answered.

"I've got Mom's car. If you like, we can go over to my house and you can take your pick of the books in the Gorman library. That is, if you don't have plans. . . ."

"Not a thing," Sarah said. He had made her feel so much better that it was all she could do to keep from hugging him. His description of scrying had made it sound like a normal, if not exactly commonplace, ability, like wiggling your ears or touching your nose with your tongue. And the thought that the horrible image she had seen in the paperweight might have been a reflection of an event from the past rather than a prediction of something that was destined to happen was extremely comforting.

She went back to her room to collect the library book and then accompanied Charlie out to the station wagon. Yowler sidled out into the yard behind them and fell into a pantherlike pose at the sight of a row of crows on a telephone wire.

That same sight snapped Sarah back to the question that was yet unanswered.

"What do you think I should do about the crow in my locker?" she asked as she settled herself in the passenger's seat and Charlie started the engine. "If nobody's willing to believe me—"

"You've got to *make* them believe you," Charlie said. "You can't just let this slide by like it never happened."

"You didn't make an issue of the fish in *your* locker."

"That wasn't the same. I didn't have to convince people. Mr. Prue could smell it all the way down the hall."

"He told me you laughed it off."

"In my case that seemed like the sensible thing. The fish was a joke, not a threat. And it wasn't an organized effort, it was done on impulse. When the guys didn't get a rise out of me, they gave up. It wasn't an escalating thing like the scaffold and the crow."

"You don't think tripping you and breaking your arm is worth mentioning?"

"That could have been done accidentally."

"Oh, Charlie," Sarah said softly, her heart aching for him.

"No sweat," Charlie said with a shrug. "Those jocks are in the habit of shoving people around. It's what they do on the football field. But the sketch and the crow are some-

167

thing different. You've got to convince your mom and Mr. Thompson to take those seriously. Certainly your mom."

A few minutes later he slowed the car and pulled into a driveway next to a small stucco house very much like the one Rosemary and Sarah were renting, except that instead of front steps this house had a ramp.

"My dad's in a wheelchair," Charlie said, anticipating the question. "I'm glad you're going to get to meet him. He doesn't get out much, and it's a special event when we have company. But I've got to warn you, he's a character, so don't let him throw you."

They got out of the car, and Charlie led the way up the walkway to the house.

As soon as they stepped through the door, the explanation for Charlie's fund of knowledge about unusual subjects became apparent. The people in this house were obviously voracious readers. One whole wall of the living room was lined with floor-to-ceiling bookshelves, and another wall held shelves to the level of a window ledge. Even the tables at either end of the sofa had shelves built into them to house tall books that wouldn't fit easily on conventional-sized shelves.

"Mom? Dad?" Charlie called. "We've got company!"

The woman Sarah had met throwing papers on the first day after Charlie's injury emerged from the kitchen, wiping her hands on a dish towel.

"Sarah!" she exclaimed. "How nice! I was wondering when Charlie was going to get around to inviting you over!"

"Don't tell me it's Sarah the Marvelous and Magnificent!" a man's voice called from the back of the house. "Am I finally going to get a look at the wondrous young

168

woman who causes our son to whistle arias as he folds his stack of papers?"

Mrs. Gorman exclaimed, "Ed, *really!*" and Charlie looked as if he wanted to sink through the floor as a bearded man in a motorized wheelchair came zooming out of a hallway that Sarah assumed led back to a den or a bedroom.

"I hope you'll forgive him, Sarah," Mrs. Gorman said apologetically. "My husband's a terrible tease. He's also a maniac driver, so be ready to leap out of the way, or you'll have bruises on your kneecaps."

"I'm sorry, Sarah, I didn't mean to embarrass you," Mr. Gorman said with a good-natured smile that was much like Charlie's. "Is it permissible to say that now that I see you in person, I'm overwhelmed by my son's good taste? And my wife is totally wrong about my skills as a driver. I assure you, you're safe in our home. Just stand close to the walls and suck in your stomach as I whiz by."

"You don't scare me," Sarah said, attempting a smile, but not quite able to pull it off. Not when confronted so suddenly with the sight of two empty trouser legs knotted at the knees to prevent them from becoming tangled in the wheels of the chair.

"Charlie didn't tell you?" Mr. Gorman asked, his voice going suddenly gentle. "Son, I just wish you'd learn that it's a kindness to totally prepare people instead of doing a halfway job of it. When you do that, they expect to find me in a leg cast. Sarah, please, don't be upset. It was just an accident at work. I assure you the condition isn't catching."

"Have you kids had lunch yet?" Mrs. Gorman asked, stepping in with practiced efficiency to redirect the conversation to a happier topic. "I have a pot of soup on the stove, and I was just getting ready to dish it up. Please, stay and join us, Sarah. Charlie tells us you're from California, but that's a massive state. Whereabouts did you live? Were you lucky enough to be by the water?"

A few minutes later Sarah found herself at the table in the Gormans' cheery blue and yellow kitchen, swallowing homemade vegetable soup and telling them all about a place called Ventura where the air smelled of salt and sea foam and the winter was heralded by orange blossoms.

chapter
SIXTEEN

"Why didn't you tell me?" Sarah asked when they were back in the station wagon headed for her house. "That bookstore that was burned down—your parents were the owners! It was your father who was burned so badly that his legs were amputated!"

"At the time it didn't seem necessary to tell you," Charlie said. "It isn't something you talk about to somebody you hardly know."

"But since then we've gotten to be friends!"

"We've had other things to talk about. And the truth is, Sarah, it's a subject that's hard for me to handle. My dad wasn't an unathletic klutz like I am; he used to play tournament tennis. And he loved to dance. He and my mom used to roll up the rugs—we had rugs back then, when we didn't have to keep the floors clear for the wheelchair— and they'd dance at night after dinner. And they wouldn't pull the shades. I sometimes think that's what made people madder than anything. Not only were my folks 'evil' because they sold unconventional books, they were 'evil' because they had unconventional fun together."

"How can they stand to keep living here?" Sarah asked him. "Your father can't work—"

"He does better than you'd think," Charlie said. "He writes book reviews for some pretty prestigious magazines. And Mom works as a bookkeeper. We manage."

"What made you suddenly decide that you wanted me to meet them?"

"It just seemed important. I wanted you to see for yourself what can happen when small-town fanatics go crazy."

"Because of the crow in my locker?"

"I want you to take that seriously."

"You don't mean that you think somebody's actually going to burn down our house!"

"We can't know what might happen," Charlie said. "There's something creepy about this town. It's like there's a boil beneath the surface, always ready to erupt. I've felt that ever since we came here."

"You mean you weren't born here?"

"I was born in Arizona," Charlie told her. "My folks had a New Age bookstore in Sedona, a town that's supposed to be a hub of psychic vibrations. Everything was going great there, when suddenly about five years ago they got this feeling that we had to come *here*. By 'here,' I mean *exactly here*—to this one particular town, this dot on the map that they'd never even heard of until they flipped through an atlas and found it. They were drawn here by some karmic force, the same way your mother was."

"Rosemary wasn't drawn here by anything but Ted," Sarah said.

"I'm sure that's what she believes."

"Why else would she have come here?"

"I just told you, my parents think they were led here by karma. That's why they didn't move away from here after the arson. They feel that one of us made a commitment before birth to perform some duty in Pine Crest, to complete some business that was left unfinished in a former lifetime."

"Your parents believe in reincarnation that strongly?" Sarah asked incredulously.

"They believe in it so strongly that my dad has forgiven the arsonists," Charlie said. "He figures that in a former lifetime he probably harmed them, and now the score's even. That's the reason he's able to joke around like he does. He doesn't feel bitter or hold grudges."

"If we've lived before, why can't we remember it?" Sarah asked him.

"Mahatma Gandhi called that nature's kindness," Charlie explained. "His theory was that everyday life would be impossible if we carried such a tremendous load of memories around with us. I'm not asking you to buy this, just don't close your mind to it. Read those books and then see how you feel about it. Once you've done that, I've got a scenario I want to run past you."

"I don't know that I want to hear it," Sarah said nervously.

"You can decide that later," Charlie said, bringing the station wagon to a stop in front of her house. "For now, though, read those books. I think you'll find them interesting."

"I will," Sarah assured him. "Thanks for lending them to me. And, please, thank your mother again for me for the great lunch."

173

Ted and Rosemary had returned from their own lunch while she was at the Gormans' and were out in the yard with Brian. Ted was busily raking the last of the oak leaves into piles, and Brian was rolling around in them like a demented puppy. Rosemary was standing on the sidelines, watching but not participating. To Sarah her mother looked a little bit lonely.

"So, there you are!" Rosemary called to her as Charlie drove off and Sarah started toward them across the yard. "We couldn't imagine where you'd gone. From the looks of that armload, you must have been to the library. Are those for your witch-hunt report?"

"I decided to switch to another subject," Sarah said. "I borrowed these books from Charlie. His dad writes book reviews, so they've got a huge library."

She saw no reason to add that the books she had borrowed from the Gormans had nothing to do with her history paper.

Ted paused to lean on his rake, seemingly undecided as to which part of her statement to attack first. It didn't take him long, though, to make up his mind. "You've been over to the Gormans'? Frankly, Sarah, I don't think that's an appropriate place for you. Charlie's a nice enough kid, despite his weight problem, but his parents are—how shall I say it?—a little bit odd."

"I liked them," Sarah said. "I think Rosemary would too." She turned to her mother. "Mrs. Gorman said she'd love to meet you. She works during the week, but she thought some weekend morning you might like to come over and have coffee. She's going to call you."

"How nice!" Rosemary said, her face lighting up with pleasure. "It's so ridiculously hard to make friends here.

The neighbors all seem so busy. They didn't even invite me in when I stopped by to introduce myself."

"I doubt that Mrs. Gorman is your type," Ted said. "Besides, don't you think our weekends should be devoted to family? Sarah, what's this about switching topics for your history paper? It seems pretty late in the game for you to do that. Isn't that paper due right after Thanksgiving?"

"I picked the wrong subject," Sarah said. "It's not working out. I'm going to do my paper on the Boston Tea Party."

Before he could pressure her further, she hurried on past him into the house.

She expected to find Kyra in the living room watching television or jabbering on the telephone, but the room was empty. As Sarah started down the hall toward her bedroom, she began to allow herself to hope that Brian was the only one of Ted's children who had come back to the house with him. When she opened the door to her room, however, that hope was vanquished by the sight of Kyra, standing at the bureau rummaging through one of the top drawers.

"What do you think you're doing?" Sarah demanded. "That happens to be *my* drawer."

Kyra froze and then turned slowly to face her.

"I was looking for my rhinestone earrings," she said. "You know—the ones Eric gave me for my birthday."

"What would they be doing in my drawer?" Sarah asked coldly.

"I couldn't find them anywhere at home," Kyra said. "Then I remembered that the last time I wore them was the night Dad took me out to dinner and I spent the night here afterward. So I thought that maybe I left them here and you found them."

"If that had been the case, I would have dumped them into one of your drawers," Sarah said. "The last thing I'd ever do is steal a pair of junky earrings with gaudy fake diamonds." Her gaze quickly took in the rest of the room. "What's my closet door doing open? Did you think you'd find your earrings on a hanger?"

"It's my closet too," Kyra shot back defensively.

"In name only! You've never kept anything in it." Sarah walked over to the closet and peered inside. "You still don't have anything in it. You weren't hanging up stuff of your own, you were rooting through my stuff!" Her eyes flew to the shelf at the back of the closet where she kept her tote bag. "You've been into my pack! It's unzipped!" She glanced down at the floor. "And my shoes! You've even been into my shoes—they're all neatly in line!" She turned back to Kyra, her eyes blazing. "If you've been into my bureau and closet, you've probably been into my locker at school! You must be the one who left the crow!"

"What crow?" Kyra asked innocently.

"Don't pretend you don't know about that!" Sarah said. "You either did it or you got your girlfriends to do it!"

"I don't know anything about any crow," Kyra insisted.

"Or the picture of the gallows that was shoved in my locker?" Sarah didn't bother to wait for a reaction. "What have you done to turn everybody at school against me!"

"I didn't have to do anything," Kyra said. "This is my hometown! I was born here! You don't belong here! Everybody knows that your mother broke up my parents' marriage. There's no way Rosemary could have done that if you hadn't bewitched my father!"

"Get out of this room!" Sarah told her, shaking with fury.

"It's my room too!" Kyra said, crossing her arms in a gesture of defiance.

"I warn you, if you stay in this room one more minute, you're going to regret it!" Sarah gestured toward the paperweight on the desk. "You know the damage I can do with *that* when I choose to! I can give you the kind of future people only know in nightmares!"

Kyra turned pale and began to back away from the bureau without even bothering to close the drawer.

"Make sure that you pass that message along to your friends," Sarah told her ominously, fueled by the astonishing effect of her ludicrous statement. "Tell them that if they do anything more to Charlie or me, I'll see that they—that they—" She searched frantically for the ultimate threat. "I'll see that they go up in flames and lose their legs exactly like poor Mr. Gorman!"

"It's true!" Kyra whispered, stumbling backward across the room. "You are just what they say you are! You're an honest-to-God witch!"

"You'd better believe it!" Sarah snarled dramatically. Dropping the books on her bed, she stalked toward Kyra with arms extended and hands contorted into claws.

With a whimper of terror Kyra whirled and bolted from the room.

Sarah shoved the door closed and sagged against it, panting from exertion, as if she had been engaged in a physical battle. She could not believe the effect that her performance had had on Kyra! The girl had actually believed Sarah was capable of putting a curse on her!

"I bet that's the last time she gets into my things," Sarah muttered victoriously. Kyra, of course, would describe the scene to her cronies, probably embellishing it so that smoke poured out of Sarah's nostrils, which would end any possibility of Sarah's forming friendships in Pine Crest. She would finish up the school year alone, except for Charlie, but she wouldn't be missing much. These weren't the kind of people she wanted for friends, and college would open the door to a whole new social life.

Now that the room was her own again, she went over to her bed and, for lack of anything better to do, picked up one of the books Charlie had loaned her. She intended only to skim it, but became so caught up in it that she was startled when Brian rapped on the door to summon her to dinner. When she arrived at the table, she was pleased, but not particularly surprised, to discover that Kyra had pleaded a headache and gone home. As soon as the meal was over and Sarah had done her share of cleaning up the kitchen, she returned to her room and plunged back into her reading.

"So what did you find out?" Cindy Morris asked eagerly.

The group of girls was gathered in the kitchen at the rectory. Cindy almost always had the house to herself on Saturday evenings, when her father conducted counseling sessions at the church and her mother presided at meetings of the Women's Auxiliary.

Kyra sat stiffly in a straight-backed chair at the end of the kitchen table, both nervous and pleased to be the center of such concentrated attention from the most popular girls in the school.

"I didn't find physical evidence," she admitted reluctantly. "I think I would have, though, if Sarah hadn't walked in on me. She seemed scared when she found me searching through her drawers."

"Oh, damn!" Debbie Rice said. "I was hoping that you might have found a rag doll with pins stuck in it or maybe a melted wax statue—something we could show to Mr. Prue or to Cindy's father."

"I don't have physical evidence," Kyra repeated. "What I do have, though, is her verbal confession that she's a witch."

"She came right out and told you!" Leanne Bush gasped.

"Not only that, but she threatened all of our lives," Kyra said. "She said for me to tell you that if we don't do exactly what she wants us to, she will—and I'm quoting her exactly—'give you the kind of future people only know in nightmares.' She vowed to set us on fire and burn us alive!"

"I told you!" Misty Lamb exclaimed, beginning to tremble. "She has powers that go beyond anything any of us can imagine! I didn't realize, though, that she was that evil and vindictive!"

"She caused your mother to get a concussion," Cindy reminded her.

"Well, yes—she did see Mom fall when she looked in the crystal."

"She didn't just see it, she made it happen! There was nobody else in the kitchen. Your mother wouldn't have gone crashing to the floor unless somebody shoved her."

"Danny and his friends have been watching her house,"

Jennifer Albritton said. "Danny said one night when the moon was full, Sarah went creeping out to cast spells on her neighbors. She paused in front of each house and put a hex on it. When she caught on to the fact that he was following her, she disappeared! She just vanished into thin air! One moment she was there, and the next she was *gone!*"

"Bucky told me that on another night, she opened her front door and stood staring out at them," Leanne said. "There was nothing to lead her to do that, she just sensed that they were there. She must have sent the black cat out to spy on them, because the minute she appeared in the doorway, it materialized out of nowhere and jumped into her arms. She cuddled it up to her face, and they whispered to each other. Her animal familiar can *talk* to her!"

Jennifer turned to Cindy. "Should we go to your father?"

"We can't do that without presenting him with evidence," Cindy said. "Our only real proof that Sarah's a witch is the way she can tell fortunes and put curses on people. If we told Dad that, we'd have to explain how we know it, which means that we'd have to confess that we got our fortunes told."

"You can't do that!" Kyra exclaimed in immediate panic. "It would get us in terrible trouble!"

"Why are *you* so upset?" Leanne asked in surprise. "Sarah never told *your* fortune."

"I was thinking about the rest of you," Kyra said hastily. "And of course I'm concerned about Eric. She cast a spell on him and forced him to assist her. From what Eric's told me, she was doing those readings in my father's apartment on Barn Street. Trespassing on private property is a criminal offense, and all of you did it when you went there. If Dad finds out about that, he'll go through the roof. I wouldn't be a bit surprised if he filed lawsuits against all of you."

"I wish you could have taped her confession," Jennifer said.

"I wasn't prepared," Kyra said. "The last thing I ever expected was that she would admit to it."

"Maybe we could get her to confess again, and this time record it—"

"That'll be the day!" Leanne said. "Can't you just imagine the conversation? 'Sarah, dear, we'd like you to walk up to this microphone and confess that you're a witch so you can be properly punished for your wrongdoings and so you and your mother can be ridden out of town on a rail.' Sure, she'll agree to that!"

"What if we don't give her a choice?" Debbie said.

"What do you mean?"

"There are ways you can force people to confess to things."

"If you're talking about physical torture, forget it," Kyra said. "I'm not going to be a part of anything like that."

"We don't need you to be a part of anything," Debbie said. "If you want to bail out, you can do it and forget you ever talked to us. I guess I was mistaken, but it was my impression that you wanted Sarah and her mother out of the picture so your dad would come back to the family."

"I do," Kyra said. "But not like that."

"Debbie didn't mean that we'd hurt her," Cindy said reassuringly. "All we would ever do would be to scare her a little. Kyra, I truly believe that's all it would take to send

181

that mother-daughter team of witches back where they came from. We just need to get Sarah someplace where we can put a little pressure on her."

"How about inviting her to the beer bust?" Leanne suggested.

"The beer bust?" Kyra repeated in bewilderment.

"The football team always throws a kegger up on the hill on the Friday after Thanksgiving," Leanne explained. "It's a secret tradition."

"She'd never come," Misty said. "Not even if we invited her."

"She would under the right circumstances," Debbie said. "That crow sent a pretty strong message. A witch who finds a dead familiar in her locker has to realize that the people she's harmed are not incapable of violence."

"Sarah mentioned a crow," Kyra said. "I didn't know what she was talking about."

"Bucky did it," Leanne said hastily. "I never even touched it."

"You touched it when you put it into her locker," Misty said.

"My *skin* didn't touch it. I wore gloves."

"That's over and done with," Cindy said. "That's not what we're here about. The issue, Kyra, is whether or not you're one of us. Leanne and I are going to be graduating in the spring, and there are going to be a couple of slots open on the cheerleading squad. The student body votes, but that's only for show; the squad and the team call the shots with word-of-mouth promotion. It's very important that we make our decision carefully. We're together all the time at practices, and we travel to out-of-town games together, and it wouldn't work out to have somebody we couldn't get along with."

"All I did was ask about the crow," Kyra said meekly.

"Like I said, that's beside the point. Are you ready to be one of us?"

Was she ready to have the dream of a lifetime come true?

"If we're only going to scare her," Kyra said, "then of course I am."

chapter
SEVENTEEN

"Have you read them yet?" Charlie asked her on Wednesday morning.

"I've read a couple of them," Sarah said, sending a newspaper soaring across a brown lawn to land precisely on a doorstep.

"Well, what was your reaction?"

"The concept is fascinating." Sarah craned her neck to look back as the door of the house opened. A woman in a terry-cloth bathrobe bent to scoop up the paper without having to step outside. "Did you see that pitch? Am I good, or am I good?"

"My wrist had better heal fast, or you're going to steal my route," Charlie said. "So, okay, the concept is fascinating. My question is, do you think there's any validity to it?"

"I'm not sure," Sarah said. "I haven't had a chance to read everything, but I was surprised and impressed by all that research. I hadn't realized so many studies had been done on people who claim to have past-life memories."

"Dr. Ian Stevenson alone has more than two thousand

cases on file at the University of Virginia," Charlie said. "In some of them young children started speaking foreign languages they had never been exposed to. How can you explain that, except that the knowledge of the languages was transferring over from former lifetimes in other countries?"

"I can't," Sarah admitted.

"That theory would also explain the existence of child prodigies like those kids who are playing piano concertos by the age of five. In a former lifetime they might have been Mozart or Beethoven, or maybe just talented people who spent their lives playing instruments."

"Why is it so important to you that I believe in this?" Sarah asked him, picking up another paper and sending it sailing out the car window. "You're not exactly the type to be an evangelist."

"It's not that I'm asking you to accept it unconditionally," Charlie said. "I just want you to accept that it's a possibility. Because, like I told you the other day, I've got a scenario I want to run past you, and I want you to be able to listen with an open mind."

"Okay, I'm listening," Sarah said.

Charlie drew a deep breath and then said slowly, "I'm starting to think it's possible that I was living in Salem in the seventeenth century at the time of the witch-hunt. That may be why I hallucinated and saw the topic 'Salem Witch Trials' as if it was printed in boldface on that handout in history class. I came into this lifetime with that subject entrenched in my subconscious. All it took to bring it to the surface was to see those words on paper at a moment when I was vulnerable."

"You've got to be joking!" Sarah had just picked up the last of the papers. Now she let the hand that held it drop

185

to her lap. "Now, I suppose, you're going to tell me you know who you were back then?"

"I think I may have been Giles Corey," Charlie said, ignoring her sarcasm. "I reacted violently to that name the first time I saw it, and when I started reading about the way Giles Corey died, I suddenly couldn't get my breath. It was like my ribs were caving in."

"He was the one who was crushed to death?"

"That's the guy," Charlie said. "In order to be tried in New England, the accused person had to speak out to answer his indictment. When he was asked, 'How will you be tried?' he was supposed to answer, 'By God and this court,' which meant he was giving permission for the court to try him. Giles Corey knew that everybody who was tried was found guilty, so he refused to open his mouth. Without his permission he couldn't be brought to trial, so they couldn't hang him for witchcraft. What they could do, though, was torture him to make him answer. He never gave in, so they crushed him to death with heavy stones. That was the turning point in the witchcraft epidemic. People suddenly snapped to how crazy things were getting, and Sir William Phips, the governor whose own wife was accused of witchcraft, issued a proclamation pardoning and releasing everybody."

"You're serious?" Sarah stared at him, too stunned to know how to react. "You actually think you were the man who put an end to the witch-hunts?"

"Actually, I do," Charlie answered, almost smiling. "Are you going to throw that paper, or are you planning to make a pet of it?"

Sarah hurled the paper without bothering to look where she was aiming. It careened to the left and landed in a bush.

186

"That's the craziest thing I ever heard!" she exploded.

"It would explain all these pounds I've been toting around with me since birth," Charlie said as if he hadn't heard her. "They're symbolic of the weight that put an end to poor Giles. You might say I came into this lifetime karmically weighted down."

"Then what about me?" Sarah demanded. "Remember, I saw that topic highlighted too! Do you take that to mean that *I* was involved in the witch-hunt?"

"That's for you to figure out," Charlie replied calmly.

"If that were the case—which it most certainly is not!— wouldn't it be sort of coincidental that the two of us would just happen to wind up in the same town, the same grade, and the same history class?"

"The whole idea of karma is that nothing is coincidental," Charlie reminded her. "Our lives are lived by a game plan that we agree to before birth. The theory is that souls that are karmically linked keep returning to this earth plane at the same time so that they can interact with each other. Did you read that book *Beyond the Ashes?*"

"I haven't gotten to that one yet," Sarah said.

"It's one of the most impressive accounts I've ever read. Over a ten-year period the author, Rabbi Gershom, counseled dozens of people who, even as very young children, had detailed memories of former lives as Jews who were executed during the Holocaust. They were all about the same age, as if they had come back together to help each other adjust to that past-life trauma."

"The Holocaust took place in Europe in the twentieth century," Sarah protested. "It didn't have anything to do with the witch-hunts in Salem."

"I don't mean to imply there's a direct connection," Charlie said hastily. "I'm just saying the concept is similar.

187

Certainly the Holocaust and the witch-hunts were very different, but both were atrocities that were rooted in group hysteria. If the witch-hunts and accompanying hangings had taken over this whole country, who knows how many innocent people might have been killed?"

"Home sweet home," Sarah said in relief as Charlie pulled up in front of her house. "I can't say this was the greatest hour I ever spent with you."

"I didn't mean to upset you," Charlie said.

"Well, you did," Sarah told him. "It's one thing to speculate about a concept like reincarnation, but it's another to say you've experienced it. It's like theorizing about where flying saucers come from compared with announcing you went for a ride on one. Are you going to insist that all the other people who took part in the witch-hunt have been reincarnated too? Is that why so many kids thought that topic was in boldface—because it triggered subconscious memories in all of them? Now I guess you want me to believe that we've got one big mass of former witches and witch-killers living in Pine Crest, because they made an agreement before birth that they were going to convene here? Charlie, give me a break!"

"I'm not going to insist on anything," Charlie said quietly. "It's obvious that I've said too much already."

"You better believe it!" Sarah opened the door and got out of the car.

"You don't have to throw papers tomorrow," Charlie called after her as she started toward the house. "Mom won't be working on Thanksgiving, so she can help me."

"Great!" Sarah shouted back at him.

"She's off the next day too, so you've got a two-day vacation, plus the weekend!"

"Quadruple great!"

"See you on Monday!" Charlie called as she hurried across the yard. Sarah didn't turn to answer him. She realized that she was hyperventilating as if she had been running a marathon. She let herself into the house, shoved the door closed behind her, and then impulsively locked it as if securing it against demons. Immediately she was struck by the absurdity of the gesture. Who or what did she think she was locking out? What in the world had gotten into her? Nobody was chasing her. The only thing that was out there was her good friend Charlie—Charlie with his self-deprecating humor and offbeat reading habits, Charlie who had accepted her story about the crow when nobody else would believe her. Just because she and Charlie had gotten to be buddies didn't mean that she had to take everything he said seriously.

Charlie was *not* Giles Corey! That idea was ludicrous! The weight problem he was so concerned about and couldn't seem to conquer was not symbolic of anything other than his basic anatomy, which was evidently different from his parents', and a passion for milk shakes!

As she took off her jacket and flung it onto the coat tree, she became conscious of the sound of the television, something she was unaccustomed to hearing in the daytime. When she went into the living room she found her mother seated on the sofa, with coffee cup in hand and an open box of doughnuts on her lap, staring at the screen. She looked as if she were mesmerized.

"What are you watching?" Sarah asked her.

Rosemary glanced up, startled.

"Oh, hi, honey! I didn't hear you come in. It's just one of those silly talk shows."

"Since when do you watch those?"

"I've just recently started," her mother said. "Actually

they're kind of amusing. These women on this panel all say they have proof Elvis Presley isn't dead, because at night he crawls in their windows. Poor old Elvis has to be pretty creaky by this time, but he makes it up their gutter spouts! Isn't that hilarious?"

"You wouldn't even consider watching this kind of stuff back home," Sarah said.

"Back there I had work and friends and meetings and all sorts of other things," Rosemary said. "Now I'm a lady of leisure—so . . ." She gestured toward the set.

Sarah walked over to the sofa and stood gazing down at her mother, giving her her full attention for the first time in weeks. There was no doubt about it, Rosemary had changed. Her eyes were dull and her face looked puffy and tired, as if she had been sleeping too little or possibly too much. She had also gained weight, which gave her a matronly look she had never had before. Much more disturbing, however, was that the aura of vitality and vibrancy that had always seemed to light up her mother from within and make her the unique individual who was Rosemary Zoltanne had vanished.

Rosemary's gaze had shifted back to the television screen.

"Mom?" Sarah said.

"What, honey?" Her mother glanced up at her, startled by the name that Sarah so seldom used.

"Why did we come here?" Sarah asked her.

"What a silly question! We came here because it's where Ted lives and has his career."

"Ventura is the place where *you* had a home and a career," Sarah said. "Weren't those as important as Ted's?" When her mother didn't respond, she continued more gently, "Truthfully, Mom, has this all turned out as you hoped it would? Are you happy here?"

Rosemary was silent a moment as if weighing the question. Then she said, "In all honesty, no. I'm not all that happy the way things are now. But I know they're going to get better once Ted and I get married."

"What's going to change if you get married, except that your name will be Thompson?" Sarah challenged her. "The truth is, I don't even think you're all that much in love with Ted. You've convinced yourself that you are. I'm not just trying to be mean, but what's there to love about him? He's bossy and boring and not even especially good-looking."

"You wouldn't understand," Rosemary said.

"Try me. Tell me, what's so special about Ted Thompson that you were willing to throw over everything that you'd worked for all your life to follow him here to Pine Crest? After all, he is still legally married, and in a small town like this one that makes you the bad guy. Is he really the reason you came here? Or was it some unexplainable compulsion and Ted was just the catalyst?"

Rosemary regarded her with bewilderment. "What are you talking about?"

"Charlie explained the concept of karma to me. He suggested that destiny sent us here, because one of us has unfinished business to complete, karmic stuff left over from a previous lifetime."

"Sarah, honey, Ted's told me that Charlie comes from a rather disturbed background," Rosemary said. "Ted explained it all after you went to bed the other night. The Gormans came to Pine Crest several years ago to open an adult bookstore. Ted said they were selling material that was terribly offensive, and the worst part was they were selling it to kids from the high school. Reverend Morris preached a sermon about it one Sunday, and the congregation blackballed the store. They refused to make any purchases there, and of course they made it off-limits to their children. When Mr. Gorman realized his business was going to go under, a mysterious fire broke out at the store. Rumor has it that he burned the place down for the insurance. Not a very savory background for Charlie. It's no wonder the poor boy has problems."

"Mr. Gorman was badly burned in the fire," Sarah said. "Both his legs had to be amputated."

"What?" Rosemary stared at her incredulously. "Ted didn't tell me that!"

"I hardly think Mr. Gorman would have been in there frantically trying to put out the fire if he'd set it himself," Sarah said. "And I don't think the Gormans could have collected much insurance. If they had, their lifestyle would be different. They wouldn't be living in that cramped little house, and Charlie wouldn't be wearing patched clothes. Ted only told you what he wanted to tell you." Swallowing her anger at Ted's fabrications and her mother's gullibility, she gestured toward the television. "Well, you'd better get back to your show. I didn't mean to interrupt you."

"This one's over anyway," her mother said. "Which means"—she glanced at her watch—"that you're already late for school. This time-consuming paper route isn't working out, Sarah. Ted and I were talking about it at breakfast. We're also very concerned about your attitude toward school. The attendance office phoned the other day to say that you've been cutting classes. I couldn't believe it! You've never done that in your life. You've always been so motivated, such a high achiever! You've changed since we came to Pine Crest; you're not the same person."

"That makes two of us," Sarah said. "You don't have to worry about my being late to school, because I'm going to stay home today. I don't feel good. I think I may be coming down with something."

Leaving her mother to the television and doughnuts, she went down the hall to her room. She had not lied. She did feel nauseated. But most of all she was filled with shame at the way she had treated Charlie. He was entitled to his own ideas, weird though they might be, and she should have felt honored rather than angered by the fact that he had chosen to share them with her. She had also been hypocritical in not openly admitting that she had found the books he had given her intriguing. It was only when Charlie had tried to make the concept personal that she had been stricken with horror and panic. The theory of reincarnation was not unacceptable in itself—but it couldn't apply to *Charlie,* and certainly not to *her!*

It hadn't been fair of her to take her reaction out on Charlie. There was no way he had deliberately set out to frighten her. He had not known about the vision she had seen in the crystal of the black-haired girl with the noose around her neck. Or about her vivid dream of being witness to a hanging. Nor did he know about the hallucination she had experienced when Kyra had phoned to persuade her to take part in the carnival. She had shoved that memory from her mind, but now it returned, crashing into her consciousness with terrifying clarity, the voice shouting, *"Guilty as charged! Away to Gallows Hill!"* at a time when she had not even heard of such a place. And then, more softly, *"Poor little Betty. The child is too fright-*

ened to remember," and her own reaction, *"Betty does remember, and she's sorry!"*

And now in her bedroom, the haven where she so often fled to escape from her problems, she had no alternative but to confront the chilling possibility that *Charlie might be right.* If she had indeed played a part in the Salem witch-hunt, the terrifying nightmares, filled with so much historical detail, could be flashbacks to her own conviction and execution. And if Pine Crest was a reconstructed stage set, filled with a cast of players, reassembled en masse from that traumatic period, it would explain why the town had seemed so familiar from the instant she first caught sight of it and why her immediate reaction had been so vehement—*This is a frightening place, and I don't want to live here!*

Having started the process, she found that she couldn't break away from it. So she took that supposition one step farther. If both she and Charlie had past-life memories buried in the depths of their subconscious, wasn't it possible that the other former victims might also?

"I can't be thinking like this!" Sarah told herself. "It's crazy!"

Despite her efforts to stop, she found herself being drawn like a fleck of metal to some gigantic invisible magnet, across the room to her desk, where the research she had done on the witchcraft trials lay neatly stacked beneath the paperweight.

She lifted the crystal ball without glancing into it and set it carefully aside. Then she picked up the papers and began to leaf through them.

At the bottom of the pile, in her last set of notes, she found what she was searching for—a list of names of the people who had been convicted of witchcraft. Over a five-month period more than two hundred victims had been imprisoned, but as a result of the courageous protest by Giles Corey, only nineteen had been executed.

Against her will, yet compelled by the same eerie force that had drawn her to the desk, Sarah read aloud the names of the "witches" who had been hanged on Gallows Hill:

Sarah Wildes, Bridget Bishop, Elizabeth How, Susanna Martin, Rebecca Nurse, George Burroughs, John Proctor, George Jacobs, John Willare, Martha Carrier, Mary Easty, Alice Parker, Ann Pudeator, Margaret Scott, Wilmot Reed, Samuel Wardwell, Mary Parker, Martha Corey, Sarah Good.

Sarah Good's five-year-old daughter, who had been questioned for only five minutes, had also been convicted of witchcraft. Torn from the arms of her mother, she had spent six months in a dungeon, where terror and isolation had driven the child insane.

As she read the little girl's name, Sarah started to shake uncontrollably.

The child had been named Dorcas.

chapter
EIGHTEEN

Thanksgiving was dreadful. Not that Sarah had expected it to be anything wonderful, but at least she had thought that it might bear some resemblance to the holiday she had known and enjoyed in the past. Instead it was a new holiday, celebrated according to Ted's dictation.

Instead of the Cornish game hens that were Rosemary's Thanksgiving specialty, Ted requested a turkey stuffed with homemade cornbread dressing. And instead of a side dish of Sarah's favorite artichoke hearts, he wanted a sweet potato casserole. Neither Rosemary nor Sarah could stand the sugary taste of sweet potatoes, and the cloying marshmallow crust that Ted wanted on top made the dish even less appetizing. Besides that, he insisted on eating at two in the afternoon, instead of at their regular dinnertime. Sarah could not imagine wanting to load her stomach with heavy food in the middle of the day, but she did so for Rosemary's sake, even though she felt like the Goodyear blimp. Her mother had put so much effort into preparing the meal that anyone would have thought they were entertaining royalty.

"If Ted wanted the same Thanksgiving he had with Sheila, maybe he should have eaten over at her place," Sarah grumbled as she scraped leftover food on the plates into the garbage disposal. "We're going to be eating turkey from now until Christmas, and then I imagine he'll want another one."

Rosemary surprised her by saying, "My sentiments exactly," and then immediately softened the statement by adding, "It's a shame that Kyra and Brian couldn't have been here, but of course I can understand why their mother would want them to be with her."

For the rest of the day Ted had the television tuned to a football game, and Rosemary sat beside him on the sofa, thumbing through magazines. Sarah considered going to a movie, if only to get out of the house, and even went so far as to put on her jacket and pick up her purse, but when she opened the door, she was struck by a wave of panic that forced her quickly to close it. By the time the movie was over, it would be dark, and what if she came home to find the Watchers waiting for her? She thought about calling Charlie to ask him to go with her, but couldn't make herself do it. How could she ask a favor when she had been so rude to him? It would be amazing if Charlie ever spoke to her again, other than to give her directions when she pitched his papers. Besides, Thanksgiving was a family day. Charlie and his "disturbed" parents were probably doing something Ted would consider sick and sordid, such as sitting together in the living room listening to music or reading "evil books."

If this was their Thanksgiving, what would Christmas be like? she asked herself miserably. Ted was sure to want Kyra and Brian to help decorate the tree and be with them when they opened his presents to them. He would insist that she and Kyra exchange gifts, and would be right there looking over her shoulder to make sure that his daughter got something nice. She would give Kyra rhinestone earrings, in memory of the pair she pretended to have lost, and Kyra would probably give her a book about crows.

She spent the rest of the day in her room listening to tapes, although several of her favorites seemed to be missing. Could Kyra have taken them? she wondered. Although Kyra wasn't above that, it didn't seem likely, since she detested all music that wasn't country. It seemed more likely that Sarah had loaned the tapes to Charlie and forgotten about it. Which brought her mind back to Charlie yet again. It was painful to realize that she had neatly disposed of her one friend in Pine Crest in a burst of irrational anger. One of her few friends *anywhere,* she corrected herself miserably. She still heard occasionally from Gillian, but seldom from Lindsay, and Jon had evaporated into nothingness after his third postcard.

The afternoon dragged by, and late in the evening her mother served turkey sandwiches, which Rosemary and Ted consumed in front of the television screen. Sarah took her own supper to her room, relieved to be able to declare the day officially over.

Friday wasn't much better. There was no school, which meant that Ted was at home all day, and since he hadn't seen Kyra and Brian on Turkey Day, he insisted on having both of them over for lunch. Brian, as usual, jabbered nonstop as he gobbled turkey salad. Rosemary did her best to keep up the other end of the conversation, while Sarah and Kyra ate in stony silence.

"Rosie, I'd like you to take Brian outside for a while," Ted said when lunch was over. "I want to have a little private talk with our girls."

"I'd like to be here for that," Rosemary told him, with her eyes on Sarah.

"I'd prefer that you not be," Ted said.

"I see no reason—" Rosemary began.

"Rosie, do as I ask, please," Ted insisted. "Why don't you and Brian take a walk uptown and browse through some stores? This is the day they start putting up Christmas decorations. You might want to look for a wreath or something for our front door."

"It's almost a month until Christmas," Rosemary protested.

"It's not a bit too early to make out a wish list," Ted said. "I bet Brian would like that, wouldn't you, son?"

"Could we go to Radio Shack?" Brian asked eagerly.

"I'm sure Rosemary would be glad to take you to Radio Shack," Ted assured him. "She's probably never taken a boy shopping before. She's going to have to start learning about the kinds of things guys like us like."

"It's okay," Sarah said to her mother, and meant it. It would be easier to deal with what was coming if Rosemary wasn't there. There was nothing worse than being lectured by Ted when her mother was either supporting him like an echo machine or making weak, ineffectual whimpers of meaningless protest.

"Are you sure?" Rosemary asked, looking worried. "I don't want to leave you if there's going to be some sort of—confrontation. It would be so much easier for everybody if you girls could be friends."

"That's exactly what we're going to talk about," Ted said. "Don't worry, Rosie, we're going to get everything ironed out. By the time you come home, we're going to be a working family unit."

That will be the day! Sarah thought, but she decided for

199

once to keep her mouth shut. No matter what Ted had to say, it wouldn't change anything as far as she was concerned. She was equally sure that nothing would change for Kyra.

Once Rosemary and Brian were gone, Ted leaned forward with his elbows on the table and proceeded to deliver the expected sermon.

"The time has come for the two of you to call a truce," he said. "We can't continue living like this. You're making all of us miserable, including yourselves. The world can't always be exactly the way you want it, and you have to adjust to the reality of my commitment to Rosemary."

"Mom can't adjust," Kyra protested.

"That's your mother's problem," Ted told her. "Sheila's a grown woman, and she needs to start behaving like one."

"She doesn't know how," Kyra said, with the first show of belligerence that Sarah had ever seen her exhibit toward her father. "You never gave her a chance to act like a grown-up when you were living at home with us. You always made all the decisions and took care of everything. Mom never had a life of her own—her whole life was you, and now that you're gone, she doesn't know what to do with herself. I'm scared that maybe she's going to turn into an alcoholic!"

"I'm not going to sit here and listen to you blame me for your mother's emotional problems," Ted said. "People have to accept responsibility for their own behavior. My marriage to your mother wasn't working. Neither of us was happy. We were separated on several occasions prior to this one."

"Those times before when you moved out, you always came back," Kyra said, her voice shaking. Sarah actually found herself beginning to feel sorry for her. "Mom thinks that you'll do that again. She's just sitting there waiting for that to happen. Every time the phone rings, she thinks it's you calling to say you're coming home."

"Well, she'd better stop waiting, because this time that isn't going to happen," Ted said emphatically. "You and Brian will always be my children, and I will always love you and support you. If things work out as I hope, I'll be granted joint custody. But I'm extremely happy with Rosemary, and I don't intend to renew my relationship with your mother."

"What if Rosemary walked out on you?" Kyra asked. "What if she took Sarah and went back to California?"

"She's not going to do that," Ted said. "Rosemary has burned all her bridges. Her life is here now, and the two of you are going to have to accept that. One of these days you're going to be stepsisters, and you have to put an end to this senseless feuding and start getting along. Sarah, that means no more lying and troublemaking. It's natural for you to be envious of Kyra's popularity, but you have to remember that she's lived here all her life, so of course she has friends. Kyra, it means that you need to make more of an effort to see that Sarah is included in things. It isn't easy to enter a new high school in your senior year, and this competition over Eric certainly hasn't helped matters. If you help Sarah meet some other nice boys, she won't feel any need to chase after another girl's boyfriend."

"So that's how it is?" Kyra asked softly.

"Yes, that's how it is," Ted answered. "Both of you have to accept it."

Sarah stared down at the table, too disgusted even to look at him. She had not spoken one word, and here he was, issuing proclamations as if he were governor of Pine Crest. It had surprised her to hear Kyra stand up to him, and she now understood the true reason for the girl's hostility. Kyra's determination to drive her and Rosemary out of Pine Crest was rooted less in personal dislike than in concern for her own mother. But that didn't make Kyra's actions any more palatable—rooting through Sarah's bureau, lying to Ted about the fortune-telling business, and possibly even depositing the crow in Sarah's locker.

She and Kyra would never be friends, no matter what Ted dictated.

Which was why she was totally flabbergasted when Kyra turned to her and asked pleasantly, "Would you like to go to a party tonight?"

"That's my girl!" Ted said approvingly, reaching over to tousle his daughter's curly hair. "That's what I had in mind, letting Sarah share in your activities. So, Sarah, what do you say?"

"What kind of party?" Sarah asked suspiciously.

"Nothing big. Just a few kids getting together at Eric's house to play games and stuff."

"No, thank you," Sarah replied, trying to keep her voice from showing her true feelings.

"Now, none of that," Ted told her. "We're through with that, remember? Of course you'll go to the party. I'll drive you over myself, or you can take your mother's car."

"Don't worry about that," Kyra said quickly. "Eric and I will come by to pick you up at eight, Sarah. And now, Dad, I've got to get home. I told Mom I wouldn't stay long. You've still got Brian here. You know how she gets during holiday time. She wants someone around."

"I remember," Ted said. "Okay, baby, get your coat and I'll drive you. I'm glad you girls have come around. This is certainly going to make life a lot easier for all of us."

After the door closed behind them, Sarah got up from the table and wandered aimlessly about the empty house, feeling more alone than she ever had felt in her life. There was nothing here that was exclusively her own, not even the room in which she slept, where Kyra was free to rummage through all her possessions. The door to the master bedroom stood open, and on a whim she went in and sat down on Rosemary's side of the bed, hoping to find some comfort in the familiar essence of her mother. It was the same queen-size bed that Rosemary had had in their old apartment, but the bedside table was now occupied by Ted's alarm clock, a copy of *Sports Illustrated,* and a pile of loose change. Her parents' wedding picture, which used to have a prominent place on her mother's dresser, had been replaced by enlarged, framed photographs of Brian and Kyra. This room was no more her mother's than her bedroom was hers.

She got up to leave and, on impulse, opened the door of the closet, almost expecting to find it filled with clothes she didn't recognize. The yellow dress her mother had purchased in San Francisco glowed like a sunflower on its hanger, surrounded by Ted's shirts, slacks, and sports jackets. Sarah had seen a reflection of that dress in Rosemary's mirror before it was ever purchased. Thanks to Charlie's reassuring explanation, that thought was no longer quite as frightening as it once had been. When she closed her eyes, she could visualize Betty Parris in the kitchen of the rectory in Salem Village, breaking an egg into a glass of water and gazing intently into it until images appeared. Little could Betty have guessed that this innocent activity would lead to a frenzied epidemic of superstitious violence!

Feeling more depressed than ever, Sarah went back to

her own room, closed the door, and sat down at her desk. The first thing she did was to pick up the paperweight and put it in a drawer. She did not want to get rid of it, because it had been her father's, but neither did she want to look into it and run the risk of seeing things—past, present, or future—that were better left unseen.

She read Charlie's notes on the Boston Tea Party, skimmed his two-year-old report, and began to draft an outline for a short paper of her own. It was not going to be very good, and she would get a low grade on it. There was no way you could toss together a paper in three days and expect it to read as though you had spent three weeks on it, but at least she wouldn't get an F. Once again she owed her salvation to Charlie.

She heard Ted's car driving up, and a little while later, Rosemary's. The television went on in the living room, and before long the smells of cooking began to permeate the house. She tried to focus her mind on the material in Charlie's notes, but found that impossible. She felt as if something terrible was looming over her, something that was about to crash down on her, but she had no idea what it was, and was afraid of finding out.

Maybe it was just that she didn't want to go to the party. She couldn't imagine why Kyra had invited her, and she knew that there was no way she would have a good time. Kyra was not her friend, and neither was Eric, and neither was anybody else in this town except Charlie. Now, when she was stuck in a situation where she needed to talk to him, she felt she didn't have the right to phone him.

Rosemary rapped on the door.

"We're having meat loaf," she said. "I bought hamburger while I was out. I figured we needed a break from light meat and dark meat."

To Sarah's relief, she did not have to make conversation at dinner, as Brian never stopped babbling about all the electronic wonders he now expected for Christmas. As soon as the meal was over, she excused herself and turned to head back to her bedroom.

"Aren't you going to help with the dishes?" Ted asked her.

"Not tonight," Rosemary said. "Remember, she has a party to get ready for. What are you going to wear, honey?"

"I've decided not to go," Sarah said. "Kyra only asked me because Ted made her. She doesn't really want me."

"That's not true," Ted said. "I didn't even know about the party. Kyra came up with that invitation on her own. She's extending an olive branch, Sarah, and I insist that you take it. Kyra can't make this work by herself. You have to meet her halfway."

The doorbell chimed.

"I'll get it!" Brian shouted, leaping up and racing to the door as if he were expecting Santa Claus.

He returned to the kitchen accompanied by Eric, who seemed to be sparkling with some sort of inner fire. Eric's face was flushed, and his amber eyes held the same glitter of excited anticipation that Sarah had seen in them the first night the two of them had gone into Ted's apartment. There was something unnatural about him—something—

"I know I'm a little early," Eric said with a smile. "I hope that's okay. I need to get back to the house before my other guests start arriving."

"I'm not ready," Sarah said.

"You look great!" His grin broadened, except that tonight Sarah didn't find it charming. His teeth were as dazzling as scalpels, and the golden glow that had seemed to encase his whole being now had a murkiness to it, as if polluted with unsavory elements. She wondered how she could ever have thought he was handsome. Now she didn't even like the idea of being near him, and the thought that she'd allowed him to kiss her was unbearable.

"All our parties here are casual," Eric explained. "Except of course for the prom. Everybody will be wearing jeans. Kyra's out in the car waiting. She's dressed just like you are."

"I'm not ready," Sarah repeated. "I'll never be ready because I don't want to go."

"Now, Sarah, I thought we'd been through all this," Ted said. He addressed himself to Eric. "Sarah thinks Kyra doesn't really want her."

"Of course she wants you!" Eric said.

"I'm not going," Sarah told him, dredging up her old stubbornness and gathering it to her like a favorite garment that had been lost in the back of a wardrobe. "Tell Kyra thanks, but I have a paper to write tonight."

"Sarah . . . ," Rosemary began in a pleading voice.

"That's okay, Mrs. Zoltanne," Eric said. "I've been faced with that problem myself. I know what it's like. We'll miss you, Sarah, but if you have a paper to write, of course that has to come first. But, please, come explain that to Kyra. I'm afraid her feelings will be hurt, and I don't want to be the middleman who brings her the message. Maybe she'll even be able to convince you to change your mind."

The next thing Sarah knew, he had hold of her arm and was steering her to the door and then out into the darkness of a night too cloudy for stars. Without a word he guided her across the yard to his car, which was parked at the curb.

To her surprise, Kyra was in the driver's seat.

"Get in back," she called across to Sarah.

"I came out to tell you that I'm not going," Sarah said, making a futile attempt to extract her arm from Eric's grasp.

"You've changed your mind again," Eric said. His voice was low and as soft as a rattler's first warning.

Before she could respond, he had the door open and was shoving her into the backseat.

"I have *not* changed my mind!" Sarah insisted loudly as Eric climbed in next to her and pulled the door closed. She started to slide across to get out on the other side and then realized that somebody else was in the backseat with them. Leanne Bush's boyfriend was blocking the far door.

"Your witchcraft days are over, Madam Zoltanne," Bucky Greeves said with a chuckle as Kyra started the engine and threw the car into gear.

NINETEEN

"Where are we going?" Sarah demanded as the car took a left turn at the end of the street and headed into the darkness of the surrounding hills.

"To a party," Eric said. "You know what a party is, don't you? It's a jolly social event where you play games and have refreshments. All work and no play might make Sarah a dull girl."

"Kyra said the party was at your house!" Sarah said, sliding forward on the seat so that she could see out the side window. "This isn't the way to anywhere! We're headed out of town!"

"Every road is the way to somewhere," Bucky said reasonably, shifting his huge body so that his knee dug painfully into her left hip. "We changed the location of the party. It's going to be somewhere else. Just sit back and enjoy the ride, because it's not going to take very long."

"Kyra," Sarah said frantically, "where are you taking me?"

"Where do you think?" Kyra asked, and then giggled.

"What's the appropriate place for people to hold parties for witches? We're going up to Garrote Hill!"

"Garrett Hill?" Sarah repeated in bewilderment. "What's up there?" Then it struck her. "That's where the football team holds their beer busts."

"Among other things," Kyra said. "You know what *garrote* means, don't you?"

"Eric's great-grandfather, Samuel Garrett, was the founder of Pine Crest."

"The hill's not called 'Garrett,' you idiot, it's called 'Garrote,' " Kyra said. "Garrote, like when you hang people. Garrote Hill is where they used to string up runaway slaves during Civil War days. That's what they used to do to witches too, isn't it, Eric?"

"Right you are, Carrot Top," Eric said. It was too dark for Sarah to see his face, but she knew that he was grinning.

Whatever this is, it can't be much worse than the dead crow, she tried to convince herself. Maybe it would be the best thing that this outlandish kidnapping was happening. Kyra and her friends had finally gone too far. Abducting Sarah was a criminal action that Kyra would not be able either to deny or to explain away. Sarah had made it clear that she was not going to Eric's party. When she'd left the house with Eric and hadn't come back, her mother must have been concerned. When Rosemary checked the coat tree in the hall and discovered that Sarah's jacket was still hanging there, she would really be worried. The next thing she would do would be to phone Eric's house, and when she was told that not only was Sarah not there but also there wasn't any party, she would finally be forced to accept the validity of Sarah's accusations. If Rosemary was still so enamored with Ted that she wouldn't consider leaving him and Pine Crest, at least she would have to agree to let Sarah return to Ventura. Sarah could live with Gillian's family until she finished high school.

Bucky had been right when he'd said that it wouldn't take long to reach their destination. The dirt road that led to the top of Garrett Hill (or "Garrote Hill," if that truly was what it was called) was shorter than Sarah had imagined, making several S-curves through a density of pine trees and emerging at a clearing where a dozen or so cars were already parked.

The party—for there did actually seem to be a party—appeared to have been in progress for some time. A bonfire was burning brightly and a keg was prominently displayed at the edge of the circle of light. Foot-stomping country music blared from a battery-operated boom box, and several couples were dancing on the hard-packed earth.

"She's here!" Kyra called as she brought the car to a stop. She opened the door on the driver's side, and the dome light went on, illuminating the car's interior.

A figure approached and bent to peer through one of the rear windows.

"The guest of honor has arrived!" Cindy Morris announced in a slightly slurred voice. "Welcome to the festivities, Madam Witch Lady!"

Eric opened the rear door on his side and got out, reaching in for Sarah's hand, and, when she wouldn't offer it, closed his own hand around her wrist. Bucky slid toward her, shoving her easily out the door, and as the group collected around her, Sarah realized it consisted almost entirely of cheerleaders and members of the football team.

Despite her resolution to remain stoic in the face of

anything they put her through, she found herself trembling as Eric pulled her forward into the firelight. Could this be the honor student, the president of the class, the brilliant, charismatic son of a respected lawyer? She remembered Kyra's statement that Eric had a dual personality, the result of his resentment of his domineering father. This was just another example of that childish behavior, Sarah tried to reassure herself. Eric enjoyed the challenge of secretly defying the man who was running his life, but he set boundaries for his rebellious behavior. He might be a crazy-making game player, but she had never seen any indication that he was violent.

Holding Sarah by her wrists, Eric and Bucky pulled her across the frozen ground to the fire. The chill of the night sliced through her thin sweater as if it were made of gauze, and she welcomed the heat that was generated by the flames.

Debbie Rice threw her arms around Danny Adams and began to sway to the music.

"Dance with me, baby!" she crooned.

"Hey!" Jennifer shouted. "Hands off! Just because your sister snagged your boyfriend doesn't give you the right to start hitting on my guy!"

Bucky jerked Sarah abruptly out of Eric's grip and crushed her against his chest, stomping his mammoth feet in time to the beat. His breath on her face was rancid with the stench of beer. Sarah suddenly realized that all of them, with the possible exception of Kyra and Eric, had been drinking heavily. She attempted to twist away from Bucky, but it was like trying to free herself from the grip of Gargantua.

"That's real music!" Kyra shouted at her over the din. "Not that creepy stuff you listen to!"

211

"What does she listen to?" Leanne asked. "I'd like to hear some witch music!"

"It just so happens that I brought some tapes with me," Kyra told her. She knelt by the tape player, and a moment later the nasal vocals of the country-western group had been replaced by the rhythmic crash of ocean waves breaking on the beach at Big Sur, accompanied by the lilt of bird calls and woodwinds.

"So that's where my tapes went!" Sarah cried accusingly. "You stole them from my room!"

"*Our* room!" Kyra reminded her. "It's my room, too, remember?" She adjusted the volume to its highest level, and Debbie began to sway back and forth in a dance of her own.

"Let's get going with the trial!" Debbie cried as she undulated to the hypnotic beat of the music. "I proclaim Sarah Zoltanne guilty of witchcraft! *What say the jury?*"

As Debbie spoke, Sarah felt her arms jerked behind her back and quickly secured there with something thin and strong that cut harshly into her skin.

"You can't do that!" Kyra objected. "It's going to leave marks! I can't tell my dad this didn't happen if she goes home with marks on her!"

Bucky laughed. "What makes you think she's going to go home?" His muscular arms tightened around Sarah as he effortlessly lifted her off her feet and carried her around to the far side of the fire. And that was when she saw it, stark in the flickering firelight, the same dreadful structure as the one in the sketch that had been left in her locker.

It's the gallows from the Halloween Carnival, she thought incredulously. *Somebody from the Drama Club must have stolen it from the prop room!*

"Let me go!" she pleaded frantically. "I've never done

anything to you! I'm not a witch, I'm just a normal person like the rest of you!"

"That's what witches always try to tell people," Bucky said.

"Now, wait a minute," Eric protested. "This is going too far. Kyra's right, this will get us into real trouble. It's one thing to give her a scare, but this could be dangerous."

Ignoring Eric as if he didn't hear him, Danny pulled free of Debbie and came over to give Bucky assistance.

"Don't try any witchcraft on us!" Cindy shrieked. "We've taken your familiar hostage!"

She lifted her hands above her head, and, to Sarah's horror, she saw that the girl was holding Yowler.

"He's not a familiar!" Sarah cried. "He's just an ordinary cat! Kyra, tell them! There's nothing magic about Yowler!"

"He talks to you!" Danny shouted. "Bucky and I saw it! We saw you whispering together! If you give us one bit of trouble, he goes in the fire!"

Sarah felt something hard being shoved beneath her feet, and when she glanced down, she saw that it was a footstool. She felt the scratch of fiber against her throat and started to struggle, then looked across at Cindy holding Yowler high above the flames, and gave in to the hands that were looping the noose around her neck.

"Confess, witch!" Cindy screamed at her.

"I'm no more a witch than you are!" Sarah sobbed. "Let me go!"

Unexpectedly she heard those words echoed by another voice—a voice that had no business being in those surroundings.

"Let her go!" Charlie shouted. "If she slips off the stool, she'll hang herself!"

213

"It's Lard Ass!" somebody yelled. "What's the blubber boy doing here? Did somebody send him an invitation?"

"He goes wherever the Witch Lady goes," Debbie said. "He's one of her familiars, like the cat!"

"Or the crow!"

"Lard Ass has his own familiar!" a male voice brayed. "His familiar's a fish!"

The roar of laughter that followed reverberated through the clearing.

"Are you out of your minds?" Charlie cried. "This looks like a lynching!"

"Isn't that what they do to witches?" someone yelled.

"Charlie!" Sarah screamed in terror. "They're going to kill me!"

"Stop this!" It was Kyra again, struggling to be heard. From where Sarah stood, teetering on the footstool, she could see Kyra with Eric beside her, frantically attempting to shove their way forward through the crowd, but the group that had gathered around the gallows was packed tight.

"You've got to let her go!" Kyra shrieked. "This isn't what we planned! You promised she wouldn't be hurt! We were just going to bring her here and scare her!"

"Shut up, you wimp!" Leanne screamed back at her. "We're doing this for you!"

"No, you're not!" Kyra wailed. "I don't know why you're doing it, but it isn't for me!" Her voice was lost in the din, and a moment later she and Eric both seemed to vanish as if sucked beneath the sea of bodies by an undertow.

Charlie was still there, however, looking wide-eyed and desperate, anchored in place at the edge of the crowd by two members of the football team, each of whom had a shoulder wedged in front of him. The crowd was now writing like the wisps of smoke that appeared in the depths of the crystal ball. Sarah realized to her amazement that they were dancing, dancing to meditation music that wasn't meant to be danced to, music that wasn't meant to be played at top volume. The ocean waves actually seemed to be crashing around them, and the sound of the oboes shrieked through the trees like wounded birds.

Sarah watched the performance with increasing horror, conscious of her precarious balance on the stool as the rope chafed the tender skin of her throat. All it would take would be for one flying foot to knock the stool out from under her, and she would be left dangling from the noose.

I've lived this before, she realized, gazing down upon the crowd and feeling the formidable energy of their excitement as it mounted in feverish anticipation of the violence to come. *I've lived this experience before, but not from the gallows. In that other time I was perched upon a pair of broad shoulders, safe from any sort of harm.*

"Push her!" Debbie screamed hysterically. "Push the witch off the platform! Somebody push her! That's what you do on Gallows Hill!"

"Stop!" Charlie shouted. "Can't you see what's happening? This isn't about Sarah Zoltanne, it's about *you*! Debbie, didn't you hear what you just called this place? You called it Gallows Hill! It's not Gallows Hill, it's Garrote Hill! Gallows Hill was in Salem!"

"Keep your mouth shut, Lard Ass, and you'll be okay," somebody told him. "You're not a witch, you're just a familiar. You're not the one we've come to the hill to punish."

Charlie managed to move back from the crowd and snatch up the tape player, adjusting the volume to a background level.

215

"Listen," he said, and this time his voice suddenly had a new sound to it, a deeper, more resonant quality, as if it were the voice of a man, not a boy. "All of you listen—did you hear what I just told Debbie? Gallows Hill was in Salem. It's where innocent people were hanged over three hundred years ago! Remember what it was like, Leanne? Reach back and remember the gallows. Remember the people around you, the people who were cheering—"

"You're crazy!" Leanne cried, continuing to sway to the monotonous beat of the surf.

"I'm not crazy at all—I'm remembering, because I was there too. We were all there. Try to remember! Don't all of you remember? Reach back and try to remember—remember how scared we all were—"

"You're crazy," Leanne said again, but she seemed to be listening.

"There was a time," Charlie said, his voice going into a singsong chant, "a time when we were gathered together before. We were gathered on Gallows Hill—remember? Innocent people, don't you remember? We tried to proclaim our innocence, but nobody listened to us. The only people they would listen to were the girls—the 'afflicted children,' who accused us of being Satan's children. But we weren't Satan's children, we were good people, just like Sarah here! We never did anything to harm anybody. It was totally unfair. Misty, don't you remember—remember the trial? Remember when they said you were using voodoo to torture 'the afflicted children'?"

Misty had now stopped dancing. The crowd had grown silent and appeared to be giving Charlie their full attention.

"It wasn't my fault," Misty said in a voice that suddenly seemed to have a soft foreign accent. "Those little girls,

Betty and Abigail, came into my kitchen. They wanted me to tell them stories from my life in the West Indies, to show them how to do little spells like make their hair curl. They wanted to look in a glass and see who they were going to marry. Then they started bringing their friends—that evil Ann Putnam—she was the one who planned it, she told them I conjured the devil and asked him to attack her."

"Ann isn't here now," Charlie said firmly. "Ann Putnam died long ago, and she hasn't returned. Ann has already suffered for the harm she did to you. Debbie, now it's your turn to remember. Put yourself back and remember what it was like to be standing in that church in front of the podium with the afflicted children lined up in front of you shouting accusations."

"Pointing and screaming," Debbie snarled. "They were telling vicious lies! They said my spirit was out of my body, torturing them, biting and scratching and tearing their eyes out! I wasn't doing anything. I was old and sick. I couldn't have hurt a fly. They threw me in prison—"

"And you died there," Charlie said quietly. "Your name was Sarah Osburn then, and you died there."

"I died there." Debbie started moaning. "Nobody would help me. I needed care and medicine, and nobody would help me."

From her point of elevation Sarah could see what Charlie was attempting to do. He was backing slowly across the clearing, and, without realizing what they were doing, the crowd was moving with him, following him away from the unstable footstool. He was making himself the center of attention instead of Sarah.

"Jennifer?" he called out.

"It wasn't fair!" Jennifer Albritton responded angrily. "I didn't even live in the village. My husband and I belonged to the congregation in Topsfield. We attended church in Salem because it was convenient. We were deeply religious! We had nothing to do with witchcraft!"

"None of us did," Charlie said reassuringly. "Every one of us was innocent. Try to think back and remember what it was like to be innocent yet be accused of evil we never committed!"

"I don't remember anything like that!" Cindy said, abruptly breaking the spell and tightening her grip upon Yowler, who was struggling in her grasp. "Can't you see what Lard Ass is doing? He's got all of you hypnotized! We thought he was just a familiar, but he's actually a wizard! He's using a wizard's magic to make you imagine things that couldn't possibly be true!"

"They *are* true!" Charlie insisted. "You were there too, Cindy. Don't you remember Dorcas? You *must* remember *Dorcas*!"

Cindy was quiet a moment, as if shocked into silence. Then she said, "Dorcas was my doll. The witch said my mother took her away and burned her."

"That's what happened in this present lifetime," Charlie said. "You named your baby doll Dorcas because somewhere deep in your subconscious you remembered a real, live Dorcas from another lifetime. In your former lifetime in Salem, Dorcas was your daughter."

"Dorcas," Cindy said softly. "Where did they take her? What did they do with my baby?"

"They convicted *her* of witchcraft," Charlie told her. "Just as you're doing now to Sarah."

"But she was only five years old! She was just a baby! They never even let me tell her goodbye!"

"Dorcas survived," Charlie said. "They didn't hang her, Cindy. They chained her up for six months, but they didn't execute her. The witch-hunt craze was over before she could be hanged. Governor William Phips put an end to the executions and ordered the release of all the convicted witches who were still in prison."

"My baby was chained in a dungeon? For half a year?" Cindy cried, breaking out of her trance. "That's worse than hanging, that's torture! I'll never believe it—*never!* Lard Ass, you're a liar—a liar and a wizard and a child of Satan!" She whirled to face the others. "He's trying to cast a spell on us! He's just as bad as Sarah! They're two of a kind!"

With a shriek of rage she threw the terrified cat at Charlie's face and then hurled herself upon him, taking him by surprise so that he stumbled and fell. As if on cue, the rest of the crowd followed suit, like rabid animals suddenly released from cages. Sarah lost sight of Charlie in the furious onslaught; all Sarah could see were bodies and flying fists.

"Dear God, please, help him," she whispered. "Please, don't let them kill him."

She felt her own darkness descending as the world grew dim and her knees began to buckle beneath her. She was going to faint, and there was nothing she could do to prevent it, and when she collapsed, she would be hanged—executed like the witch she must be to have drawn this dear, good person into such a nightmare and caused the terrible violence that now filled the clearing.

"Please, help him," she murmured again.

And to her astonishment somebody responded to her prayer.

"What do you think you're doing!" a man's voice bellowed. "Has every one of you gone crazy? Back off and let me see what you've done to these poor kids!"

It's Governor Phips, Sarah thought, hovering between lifetimes, and then, just before she lost consciousness, she realized that it was Ted Thompson who was removing the noose from her neck and lowering her into the upraised arms of her mother.

chapter
TWENTY

Sarah set the vase of flowers on the windowsill of the hospital room before turning her gaze apprehensively to the boy in the bed.

He did not look as bad as she had anticipated. His head was bandaged, and an inverted plastic bag was dripping clear liquid into a tube that was attached to one arm, but the eyes that gazed back at her were bright, and the face, though smudged with yellowing bruises, was unmistakably Charlie's.

"How did you know where to find me?" Sarah asked him.

"I looked in my crystal ball," Charlie answered. He started to chuckle and then winced. "I guess it's not smart to laugh when your ribs are broken. The truth is, I couldn't stand having you mad at me, and I wanted to straighten things out. I thought if I phoned you, you'd hang up on me, so I decided to drive over to your place and try to patch things up in person. When I turned onto Windsor Street, I caught sight of Eric's car driving off, with you in it, and that seemed odd, because I'd thought you were finished with Eric."

"I was," Sarah said. "I *am.*"

"All of a sudden I wasn't sure, and I guess—I guess maybe it was jealousy or something." He flushed with obvious embarrassment. "Anyway I decided to follow you to see where you were going, and when the car started up Garrote Hill, I began to get worried, because that's where they throw those wild parties and some bad stuff goes on there. I couldn't imagine you going to a kegger with Eric, not after everything that had happened, so I fell back so that he wouldn't notice my headlights and kept on tailing him. That's how I got there—real simple. All it took was four wheels."

"What you did when you got there was anything *but* simple," Sarah said. "I couldn't believe it when you started telling them about Salem."

"I was trying to buy time," Charlie told her. "Like I said, I hung back, and by the time I pulled into the parking area, all hell had broken loose. They had you up on that footstool, and Cindy Morris was slinging your cat around, and the way everybody was screaming and milling around, I thought I'd walked into a scene from a novel by Stephen King. When Eric and Kyra couldn't break things up, they took off in Eric's car, and I gave them the benefit of the doubt and figured they were going to get help. I knew that I couldn't control things for very long, I just hoped it would be long enough for them to call in reinforcements."

"The way you got everyone to listen to you—"

"It's not hard to trigger mass hypnosis in a setting like that," Charlie explained. "Those kids had already almost worked themselves into a trance state. The music and flickering firelight had a lot to do with it, and of course they'd all been drinking. And I think they were karmically ready for it. They needed to mentally relive that nightmare in Salem so that they could put that lifetime behind them and get on with the job of becoming their true selves in this lifetime. They are probably all pretty normal people, except for Debbie. That girl needs help, but hopefully not from Mr. Lamb."

"I can't believe that none of them remember it," Sarah said. "At least that's what they all say. Everything that happened on the hill that night is a blank to them."

"It's possible that's true," Charlie said. "They were pretty well sloshed, and past-life regression can be traumatic. Poison from events that are buried in the subconscious can pour out like pus from a festering wound. Psychologists use that for healing, but a lot of people aren't ready for it, so they block it out afterward. The relief from the pressure is there, but they don't realize why."

"How did you know how to do it?" Sarah asked him.

"The weight-loss hypnosis tapes taught me the basics, and I told you my mom let me practice on her so she'd stop smoking. I regressed her back to a lifetime when she was the Marlboro Man, and that was the end of her awful habit."

"You're making that up!" Sarah said accusingly. "Don't you ever stop joking, even when you're in a hospital bed?"

"Fat people joke," Charlie said. "It's part of our defense system."

"You don't ever have to defend yourself against me," Sarah told him. "And actually"—she leaned closer to study his face—"Charlie, I think you've lost weight!"

"Already?" Charlie asked in surprise.

"Already," Sarah said, as astonished as he was. For the first time since she had known him, she could see the faint outline of his cheekbones.

"How about that!" Charlie exclaimed in delight, reaching up self-consciously to finger his jawline. "I hoped it might happen once I completed my karma as Giles Corey, but I didn't think it would be this fast. Give me another week, and I may be as lean and handsome as Eric Garrett."

"Bite your tongue!" Sarah said.

"That's *my* line."

"Well, now it's mine. If you start resembling Eric, you're out of my life."

"He's not all that bad," Charlie said. "And neither is Kyra. They're not evil kids, either one of them. They're just messed up, because of their messed-up parents. As it turned out, by bringing Mr. Thompson to the rescue, they may have saved both our lives."

"Eric has Ted convinced that it was only a hazing," Sarah said. "He explained it was sort of an initiation ceremony to make me part of the 'in' group, and it got out of hand. Of course Ted wants to believe that, and so do the other parents, and I couldn't see anything to be gained by trying to refute it. Everybody blames what happened on the liquor. The football team is in trouble at school for breaking training, and a lot of the kids got grounded, and from what I hear, the Reverend Morris is planning to preach a sermon on the evils of alcohol. Other than for that, it's like the whole thing is already history."

"Which it is," Charlie said. "Twice over—first the premiere and now the rerun. Except that a couple of centuries went by between the showings."

"I've been trying to put the pieces together," Sarah said.

"I'm willing to accept that you may have been Giles Corey, because it was his courage that ended the witch-hunt in Salem, and it was yours that ended it here in Pine Crest. And if Cindy was Sarah Good, that would explain her weird obsession with the doll she named Dorcas. And, I have to admit, the other cheerleaders did respond to hypnosis as if they were victims of the witch-hunt, although I suppose it's possible they were mimicking each other the way the 'afflicted children' did in Salem."

"What I can't figure out is how *you* fit in," Charlie said. "You must have played an important role in that past time, or they wouldn't all have ganged up on you in this lifetime."

"I know who I was," Sarah said. "In that other lifetime I was one of the 'afflicted children.'"

"What makes you think that?" Charlie asked her.

"I know it from my dreams. The visions I saw in the crystal ball were of the future, but my dreams were memories of the past, and all of those dreams were experienced from the viewpoint of a child. The victims had reason to hate me. *I triggered the witch-hunt!*"

"You couldn't have been Ann Putnam," Charlie said, frowning. "Ann received her punishment in her own lifetime. She was excommunicated, which was a fate worse than death in Salem Village, and then she became a semi-invalid. Before she died, she was finally granted Communion, but only after she delivered a public confession and begged God's forgiveness."

"I know," Sarah said. "And it was that way with most of the others. In general the 'afflicted children' led miserable lives. All except for Betty Parris. Betty didn't even get a slap on the wrist. Her father sent her to Boston to live with relatives, and she had a happy childhood and a wonderful life. Don't the rules of karma say that what goes around comes around? If we don't pay our debts in one lifetime, we pay them in another?"

"Betty was only nine years old," Charlie protested.

"That's not too young to take responsibility for your actions. It was Betty who started the witch-hunt, and Betty who could have stopped it. All she had to do was confess to her father."

"Who may or may not have believed her," Charlie said.

"We can't second-guess the past, we can only learn from it. How did your mother react to Eric's story about the hazing?"

"She didn't buy it," Sarah told him. "She took one look at that gallows and announced, 'We're out of here!' Rosemary and I are moving back to Ventura. She's already made arrangements to have our furniture shipped as soon as we find a new apartment. And the great thing is that she's been able to get her old job back! She'll be teaching at a different grade level, but at least it will be at the same school."

"What about Mr. Thompson?"

"She seems to have lost all interest in him," Sarah said. "She says he can follow us if he wants to, but she doesn't seem concerned about it. Just like flicking a switch, she's become the old Rosemary. It's like she just can't wait to take control of her life again."

"It's the same with my folks," Charlie said. "Now that our karma has been satisfied, they're making plans to leave Pine Crest as soon as I graduate. Dad says he wants to open another bookstore, but he isn't sure where yet."

"I'm going to miss you," Sarah said.

"When you see me again, I'll be skinny."

"I don't know that I want you to be skinny. I've gotten kind of used to you."

She leaned over the bed to plant a goodbye kiss on his cheek. Instead he reached up and cupped her head in his left hand, so that he was in charge of her kiss and it landed on his lips. It was not, as she would have expected, the fumbling kiss of a boy who was unused to dating but the practiced kiss of a man who knew exactly what he was doing.

Charlie released her head and smiled at her astonishment.

"In one of my former lifetimes I was Casanova," he said. "I'll tell you about it when I visit you. Or maybe it would be better to save it for the cruise ship?"

"The choice is yours," Sarah said, trying to keep her voice steady and having a hard time doing it. She drew a long breath to stabilize herself and reached into her purse. "I brought you a little memento to make sure you don't forget me."

"Fat chance of that," Charlie said.

"Stop trying to be funny."

She took out the crystal paperweight and placed it on the windowsill next to the flowers. Sunlight streamed through it, throwing rainbows on the sheets of Charlie's bed.

It was clear and transparent as window glass.

Suggestions for Further Reading

This work of fiction introduces several subjects with which readers may not be familiar. Those who wish to delve further into these topics may find the following reading list helpful. If these books are not available at your local library, you can request that your librarian acquire them through interlibrary loan.

The Salem Witchcraft Trials

The Salem Witchcraft Trials, by Karen Zeinert. (Venture Books, 1989)

A Break with Charity: A Story About the Salem Witch Trials, by Ann Rinaldi. (Harco, 1992)

Witches' Children: A Story of Salem, by Patricia Clapp. (Viking, 1987)

ESP and Other Forms of Psychic Phenomena

Psychic Connections: A Journey into the Mysterious World of Psi, by Lois Duncan and William Roll, Ph.D. This book, based on laboratory research and documented case histories, introduces young adult readers to the fascinating world of parapsychology. (Delacorte, 1995)

Past-Life Regression

Beyond the Ashes, by Rabbi Yanossan Gershom. Gershom has based his book upon the past-life memories of people he counseled over a period of ten years who, as young children, seem to have had vivid and detailed recollections of former lives as Jews who were executed during the Holocaust. (A.R.E. Press, 1992)

Many Lives, Many Masters, by Brian L. Weiss. The true account of a traditional psychotherapist whose patient began recalling past-life traumas that seemed to hold the key to her recurring nightmares and anxiety attacks. (Simon & Shuster, 1988)

Children Who Remember Previous Lives, by Ian Stevenson. A description of the author's research on children who seem to remember a previous lifetime. Stevenson explains the way he conducted the research, the results obtained, and his conclusions. (University Press of Virginia, 1987)

Mission to Millboro, by Marge Rieder. The true account of a group of present-day Californians who, under hypnosis, identified a village in Civil War Virginia as the scene of a prior life together. (Blue Dolphin Publishing, 1992)

About the Author

Lois Duncan has written highly acclaimed works of fiction for young people that include *Daughters of Eve, Don't Look Behind You, The Third Eye, The Twisted Window, Down a Dark Hall, Locked in Time, Killing Mr. Griffin, Ransom, Stranger with My Face,* and *Summer of Fear.* She is also the author of the nonfiction books *Who Killed My Daughter?*, the story of her search for her daughter's murderer, and *Psychic Connections: A Journey into the Mysterious World of Psi,* written with William Roll, Ph.D. Lois Duncan received the Margaret A. Edwards Award, sponsored by *School Library Journal* and the American Library Association's Young Adult Library Services Association (YALSA). She lives in North Carolina.

For those who would like to visit with Lois Duncan and her family on the Internet, the website address for their home page is

http://www.iag.net/~barq/